Paperback: 978-1-7375919-0-0

First paperback edition July 2021

Edited by Kimberly Leiva
Illustrations by E. M. Leiva
Cover by KDP
Published by Guillermo Leiva

Printed in the USA.

The

Stanchess

E. M. Leiva

Dedicated to my sister,

Alison,

for always being there for me.

Acknowledgments

Lots of people have helped me on the way to completing my book. I would like to thank my dad for helping me with technology and giving me the idea of publishing *The Stanchess*. A special thanks to my mom for editing my book and sitting there with me as we went over it. Of course, thank you to my sister for always encouraging me. Thanks to Siena, Charlotte, Melody, Annie and Maddy for being great friends to me, especially to Charlotte and Siena for being the first people to read *The Stanchess* and giving me advice on how to write it. Thank you to my grandmother for reading my book when I sent it to you, and thanks to my great grandmother for pre-ordering *The Stanchess*.

Many books have inspired me into writing *The Stanchess* such as Chris Colfher, the author of *The Land Of Stories*. In *The Stanchess* some parts are inspired by *The Land Of Stories*.

Hamlin's powers are also almost completely based on the character Emily, in *Pegasus* by Kate O'Hearn. I am grateful to Kate O'Hearn for this idea.

Amulet, Harry Potter, The Lion the Witch and the Wardrobe, Warriors, Wings of fire, Pegasus, Percy Jackson and *The Land of Stories*, are just a few of the books that have inspired me.

Chris Colfer, J.K Rowling, C.S Lewis, Erin Hunter, Tui T. Sutherland, Kate O'Hearn, Rick Roridan and Kazu Kibushi: I have never met you, but your books have inspired me beyond anything else.

The Stanchess

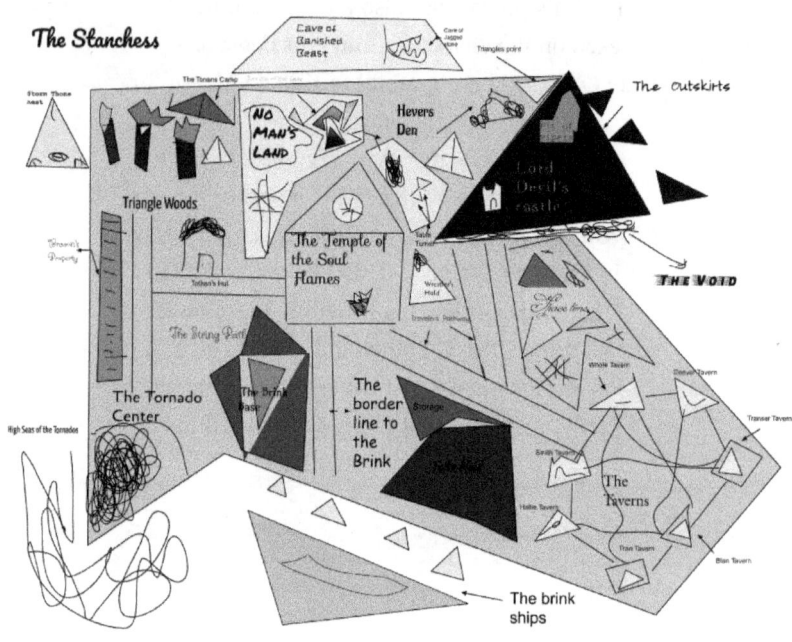

The Outskirts

THE VOID

The brink ships

The Outskirts

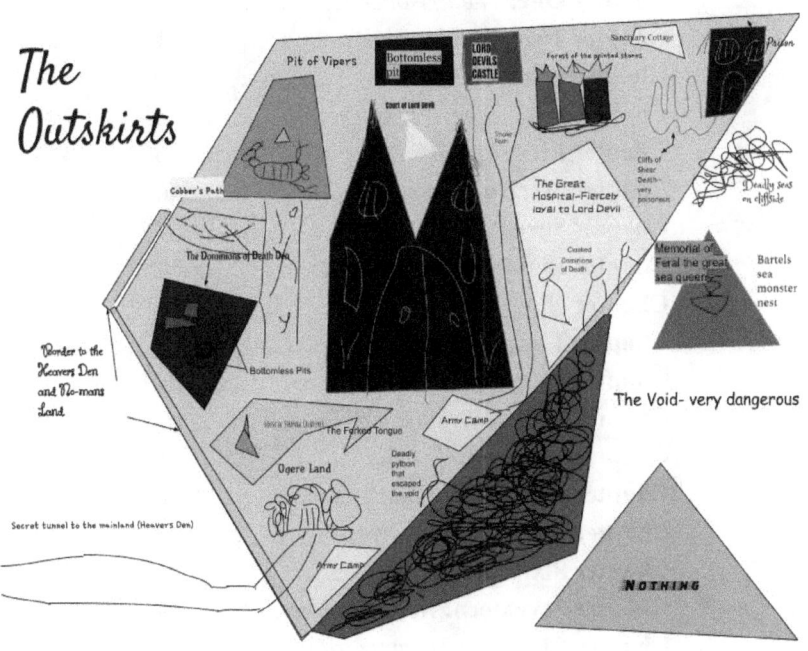

Pit of Vipers

Bottomless pit

LORD DEVIL'S CASTLE

Court of Lord Devil

Forest of the pointed stones.

Sanctuary Cottage

Prison

Cobber's Path

Deadly seas on cliffside

Cliffs of Sheer Death- very poisonous

The Great Hospital- Fiercely loyal to Lord Devil

The Dominions of Death Den

Crooked Dominions of Death

Memorial of Feral the great sea queen

Bartels sea monster nest

Border to the Heavens Den and No-mans Land

Bottomless Pits

The Forked Tongue

Army Camp

The Void- very dangerous

Ogere Land

Deadly python that escaped the void

Secret tunnel to the mainland (Heavens Den)

Army Camp

NOTHING

5

Table of Contents

Chapter One
The Prisoner

On the eve of the foul moon, a dark shadow made his way across Triangle woods. The shadow glided over fallen leaves, not making a sound. The shadow made for a dark opening in the ground below.

The shadow crept quietly into the opening until he came to a set of big double doors. Instead of knocking, he flattened himself to the ground and slipped through the gap between the floor and door.

Three guards sprang from their post. The guards carried spears and wore armor packed with velvet, their faces obscured by heavy helmets. The guards raised their spears in an X blocking his path.

The shadow threw back his sleeve, revealing an image burned into his skin, fire burned in the shadows veins. How dare they not know who he was!

"All right," the guard surrendered gruffly, "Come with me." Breathing heavily, the shadow allowed the guard to escort him down deeper.

They walked down a narrow hallway. As the shadow and his escort walked down the dimly lit hallways, guards whispered to each other. The shadow heard a guard whisper to another: "Devil, got a nasty streak there. Mother imprisoned, I heard!" Devil gave the guard a nasty look and continued on his way.

After about a quarter of a mile, they came to a small door partly covered in ivy and padlocked tight. The guard took out a small key. The little door opened a crack and they slipped in. Instantly, a dozen jail cells sprang up and the guard that had accompanied the shadow to the jail saluted to the shadow and disappeared into the doorway. All of Devil's heart skipped a beat. After all these years, he would see her.

Devil saw an iron gate with a red ribbon tied around the bars and with an extra guard to maximize security. Devil growled to the guard, "I need to speak with her."

"Do you have a pass?" the private guard questioned.

Devil pulled up his sleeve revealing his brand.

"Very well, you may go in," the private guard sniffed. He turned to face the bars, waiting for them to be raised. The guard hesitated, but finally raised the bars and permitted the shadow to pass through them into a dark, narrow, passageway where another set of bars were raised.

After what seemed like hours to Devil, he came to a small cell with only a tiny window on the ceiling to light the room. The only furniture in the room was a small metal bed with a single blanket and what looked like a pile of rags. A copper chain ran across the floor and into the pile of rags. A rotten stool with a few moldy crumbs on it was the only other piece of furniture that was in the room. Suddenly, the thing that Devil had mistaken for rags slowly sat up.

"You thought I was done with you. You thought wrong," Devil breathed.

"Hello, Son," Devil's mother greeted him coolly.

"Why are you here?" the mother inquired.

"You arrogant hag! I saved you!" Devil cried.

"You pulled me into this horrible place," Devil's Mother replied calmly.

"You rather be there than here?!" Devil roared, anger pulsing in his veins.

Quick as lightning, he crossed the cell to his mother and kicked her in the stomach. His mother groaned and doubled over.

Devil leaned over and whispered in his mother's ear, "Just do it, and I will leave."

"Never!" spat his mother.

"Very well, I will leave you to rot," Devil sneered. He turned to leave.

"Wait! I'll-I'll do it." Devil's mother choked.

Devil turned around with a smile curling on his lips.

Chapter Two
Spook Woods

Mike Lukowski rolled over. His head was throbbing from lack of sleep.

Mike groaned and checked the clock. It was half past seven; it was time to go to school. Still, he hit the snooze button. His lids felt too heavy to open, as if they were glued shut.

He hadn't slept much. He had gone to bed at nearly twelve, kept awake by a new dog barking in their neighborhood. The thing was such a pain. Mike's neighbors were hardly able to keep the dog under control, much less *train* it. The poor thing had been shut out most of the night and was howling all night, keeping all of the neighborhood up.

"Mike! For God's sake, GET UP!" his mother screamed from downstairs. Her voice seemed to pierce his head like a dark needle.

He rolled himself out of bed. Mike was thirteen years old with messy brown hair and light blue eyes. His bedroom reflected his age when he was ten; it had been covered in posters of dragons, but now it reflected his middle school life. Messy papers cluttered the floor and books were piled up on his rickety desk.

Mike mumbled to himself as he got dressed and brushed his teeth. He thudded down the stairs blinking sleep from his eyes.

"Hurry up!" snapped his mom as soon as he thumped down the stairs.

His mom was waiting for him. She had sharp features with a tight bun twisted up on her head. She always said she was inhuman.

"Get your brother. You have to leave," ordered Mrs. Lukowski.

"Good morning to you, too," muttered Mike.

"What was that?" asked Mrs. Lukowski.

"Nothing," mumbled Mike, guilty.

"CAND!" he hollered.

"WHAT!?" Mike's brother hollered back.

"TIME TO GO!"

"OK!"

Cand bounded down the stairs. He had light brown hair like his brother and was short and scrawny. He wore a light blue shirt that was tucked in.

They both grabbed a muffin and prepared to leave.

"Be safe!" called Mrs. Lukowski as they walked out the door.

"Can we go the exciting route?" asked Cand as he shouldered his backpack.

"No," replied Mike firmly.

"Why not????" pleaded Cand.

"Nope."

This conversation conditioned much of the walk to school. They went down the dark alleyway that always gave Mike the creeps.

"What's up, Lukowski?" a voice asked.

Robert Hown loomed out of the shadows, his stocky shape was crooked and his small beady eyes were squinted.

The rest of his gang loomed out. Mike just sighed. "Leave us alone, Hown."

"Is little Lukowski scared?!?" mocked Hown.

"Hey! Don't talk to my brother like that!" snapped Cand bravely.

Hown pressed a buff hand on Mike's chest. "I'll give you ten seconds to scram or I'll beat the stuffing out of you," snarled Hown.

Mike took the warning, grabbed Cand's hand and they sprinted out of the alleyway.

Mike vered away and pulled Cand into the forest called Spook Woods. He shuddered as the canopy of trees seemed to engulf him. Thick gnarled roots poked up from the earth but they just kept running.

That's when Mike remembered the legend. It was some sort of joke in the Hillside Valley, but many people took it seriously.

The legend went something like this: *Apparently, there were two children with the names Eva and her brother Eiljah. They liked to explore and sometimes their 'adventures' took them a little too far.*

They decided one day to explore Spook Woods or Dew Woods as it had been called that day. The woods rested on the coast of their town.

And for some random reason, nobody ever went in it.

Eva and Eiljah went in, but they didn't know that they were being closely followed by a young boy called Flint. Soon Eva and Eiljah got hopelessly lost in the woods. And it wasn't long before they were separated.

Flint had watched as Eiljah, while searching for his sister, entered an old abandoned house with wood so old it looked like the briefest wind could shatter the whole place.

Not soon after Eiljah entered, Eva went in. According to legend, she seemed flustered and scared even.

Flint waited a moment before following them in. The abandoned house was dark and no sound came. As soon as Flint's eyes adjusted, he wished they hadn't.

Tothan, who was an old hermit that nobody ever saw, was there too. He was standing over Eva holding a spear, with what seemed to be blood on it.

And Eva was kneeling over the broken body of her brother. He was very clearly dead. Eva seemed to be sobbing while Tothan just stood there.

A man appeared out of the shadows. He was wearing a 6-piece suit, he had a long beard and was around thirty.

"The humans will come. You must capture the gorgelina. Do it now or all you love will perish," the man spoke to Eva.

"I will never listen to you, Devil. Thrisa shall never be contained. I am the last sorcerer!" Eva had yelled at the odd man.

"Then you are a fool." The man had made an odd gesture with his hands and was gone.

Tothan took one last look at Eva and promptly disappeared.

Before Eva disappeared, many people swore she had muttered, "Run, Janalas, run. They will come for you." And then Eva disappeared, taking her brother with her.

And Flint was never seen again.

The legend replayed in Mike's mind as he sprinted through the forest. Suddenly he collided into something hard.

"Mike! What are you doing here!" gasped a voice.

Mike looked up to his best friends. Liva and Kirk were right in front of his eyes. Liva had dark black hair and green eyes; she wore jeans and a purple t-shirt. Kirk was a redhead. He had brown eyes and wore jeans as well. He was tall for his age.

"What are *you* doing here!" countered Mike.

Kirk rolled his eyes. "My mum, she was all like, 'fresh air strengthens the mind.' I went just so she would stop nagging me."

"And I wouldn't let this guy go alone," explained Liva as she shoved Kirk playfully.

"Ya guys done? We have something called school," snapped Cand.

"I know a quicker way," assured Liva.

"Enlighten us," Cand mumbled.

"Come with me."

The four friends started walking away with Liva in the lead.

Suddenly, Mike heard a twig snap behind him. He whirled around but saw nothing. He whipped his head around but still saw nothing.

"Mike, what is it?" asked Liva.

"Dunno, I thought I saw something," he replied.

"Hey! Look!" cried Cand. He pointed out something in the distance. He plunged forward.

"Cand, NO!" shouted Mike, but his calls fell on deaf ears.

Mike sighed, and he and his friends plunged after Cand. Finally, they caught up with each other. "Cand…." gasped Mike as he gripped a stitch in his side.

"Hello, Mike," greeted a prompt voice.

"Whu," Mike gasped.

Mike looked up into the face of a middle aged man. The man wore a simple black cloak with the hood down to reveal his features. His face was smooth and his green eyes twinkled.

"Liva! Kirk!" Mike called, never taking his eyes off the man.

"What is it?" asked Kirk as he thundered up beside him.

"Um, hi?" Liva said, almost asking.

"Hello, my name is Flint," introduced Flint.

"FLINT!" the children cried in unison.

"Yes," the man replied casually.

"And I have something to tell you," Flint announced.

"Back up!" demanded Liva. "Flint is a common name, so you're not in the legend, right?"

Flint barked a laugh. "Liva, isn't it? You are smarter than that. You know I'm the one in the legend."

Liva looked like she had been kicked in the stomach.

"Hey! The legends are not real!" Kirk spoke up.

Flint looked down mournfully at Kirk "Live well, son."

"Um, ok," Kirk said with uncertainty.

Suddenly a great change came over Flint's face. "Run! He's here!" Flint gasped.

Suddenly a silhouette of a man appeared. "This isn't your place, Lord Devil. It's my home!" snarled Flint at the man.

The man looked exactly the way the man with the 6-piece suit had looked in the legend.

"Quiet, I am not here for you," the man rasped.

All the children were gawking. They had just seen a man appear out of thin air.

"Not possible, not possible," these thoughts circled in Mike's head.

Suddenly the man lurched past Flint and grabbed Cand.

"CAND!" shouted Mike, snapping out of his trance. But it was too late. The man drew a knife and slit it across Flint's throat. Ruby red danced in front of Mike's eyes and Flint crumpled to the ground.

Mike made a wild grab for his brother, but the man turned on the spot and he was gone,

leaving no trace. Even Flint's body was gone
and, if he was dead or alive, Mike didn't know.

Chapter Three
Lost

"Cand," gasped Mike.

"Um, does everyone agree that that was literally impossible?" Kirk reprimanded.

"Wow, it's weird that we are all in the same dream." Liva stared into space with a dreamy expression on her face.

For some reason, Mike didn't believe they were in a dream. He shook his head and cried, "We have to find Cand!"

"Um, obviously," Kirk stated. "We'll help, but I don't know how that could be possible."

"I don't care! My brother literally just got kidnapped!" snapped Mike.

"Guys, did you hear that?" Liva asked, playing no part in the earlier conversation.

"No," Kirk and Mike said together.

Suddenly a large shape burst from the bushes surrounding them. The shape was magnificent: it had the body of a lion with deep gold fur; it had long curved talons of an eagle. But it had the head of a normal, but beautiful, young woman. But the most magnificent part

26

was the wings. Two beautiful wings protruded from her lion's back; the wings were pure white.

The shape flexed her talons.

"Thoran! Come, I think I found them!`` The shape called. Her voice was high but low at the same time.

"You better. Thrisa, we have to leave soon," called a gruff voice.

An old woman burst from the bushes. She wore a long black cloak and had short but messy gray hair, her hands shook from keratosis.

"Who are you?" demanded Mike.

"Who are YOU!" countered Thrisa and burst into a fit of giggles.

"Seriously, this can't be happening," Kirk mumbled.

He walked over to Thrisa and began pulling on her wings as though expecting them to pop off.

Suddenly Thrisa reared. She slashed her claws through the air, causing Kirk to lose his balance and crash to the ground while Thrisa landed on top of him, her talons inches from his chest.

"I assure you, young man, she is very real," growled the woman. "My name is Thoran."

"How does that help us?" snapped Kirk very defensively. Mike would have joined in, but he was too dazed to think.

"Ok, we get that! You're real!" Liva gasped as Thrisa brought her talons even closer to Kirk's chest.

"Not," muttered Kirk. Thrisa growled and showed off her talons.

"Let him go," Mike ordered in a flat, toneless voice.

Thrisa immediately stepped off his body and began licking her foot. "What?" she asked when she caught everyone staring at her.

Thoran rolled her eyes. "You done?" she asked grumpily.

"But who ARE you?" repeated Kirk.

Thrisa shifted nervously from foot to foot. "Thoran, we don't have time for this," she groaned. Her voice seemed strained.

Thoran nodded, but it seemed forced as if she would rather not do it. "Look, Mike, the world is a lot bigger than you think it is." Thoran told him, her voice low and soft.

"You mean like space?" inquired Liva.

"No," reprimanded Thrisa. "How small are your brains?"

"Look, we aren't human," Thoran growled, ignoring Thrisa.

"Yeah, I think we got that part," Kirk sighed. His forehead was furrowed and he looked like he was deep in thought.

For some reason it didn't surprise Mike. he felt like his world was shifting below his feet. His compatriots looked much more uneasy than him.

"Just tell me how to find Cand," Mike ordered, his tone quivering with every syllable.

"And us," added Liva.

Mike started to shake his head, but Thoran cut her off. "What you need to know, kid, is that we come from a world called the Stanchess," explained Thoran in a slow tone, but it did nothing to help Mike's confusion.

"The Stanchess," Mike repeated. The word rolled off his tongue like butter. It seemed so unusual, so unnatural.

"The Stanchess is in danger because of a man calling himself Lord Devil," Thrisa explained in the same slow tone as Thoran.

Kirk snorted. "That's what he's calling himself? I mean seriously?"

Mike would have laughed at the ridiculous name as well, but he felt too numb to do so.

"Yeah," Thoran sighed as if she was agreeing. But with Thoran's prickly personality, Mike didn't think so.

"And the sticken guy thinks that the Outskirts are his!" exploded Thrisa angrily.

Liva raised one eyebrow. "Outskirts?" she inquired.

"Like our underworld," Thrisa chirped. When no one seemed to get it, she continued: "You know, like the darkest spot, where all the monsters come from."

"Huh," Mike's voice still sounded flat, and he took in the information like a robot.

"Thrisa, we need to tell them," Thoran urged.

"Ok!" Thrisa spread her wings and flew to the very top branch of one of the trees. Mike wondered what one of the townspeople would think if they saw her perched there like an overgrown bird.

"Listen closely, I'm only saying this once," gushed Thoran and she began:

"When the Devil has brought fire and pain to the land
Bring the humans, bring the humans
Go to the hag of leaves
Look for the gem
When the devil has brought fire and pain to the land

31

Bring the humans, bring the humans
But beware of the cave for secrets lurk
within
Seek the three t's, find them and harness
their power
Find the girl of the souls with the fire deep
inside her
For where love is fire and where love is
betrayal.
Collect the team
But beware of the pup
When the Devil has brought fire and pain
to the land
Bring the humans, bring the humans"

"What the heck is that supposed to mean?" demanded Kirk.

"Easy, we need you to help us," Thrisa laughed as she swooped down from her branch.

"N-no, there must be some sort of mistake!" stuttered Liva. Kirk nodded in agreement.

Mike only had one question: "Why us?" he asked.

Thoran looked at him. Her gaze seemed to be burning into him. "The Stanchess calls you. Natone told me herself."

"Who's Natone?" asked Kirk.

"The hag of leaves. She lives in m-my brother, Tothan's old place, she-" Thoran was cut of by Liva.

"Wait, you mean like The Tothan, like the one in the legend?" she demanded.

"Yes, that's him. Anyway, Natone delivers prophecies and this is what she told me, so we're stuck with it." Thoran admitted.

"The three t's, it's me, Thoran and Tothan," Thrisa put in.

"The girl with the Soul Flames inside her is Hamlin. She is the daughter of Natone," Thoran added.

"Still doesn't make sense. There's too many loose ends," complained Kirk.

"Thoran, tell 'em'" Thrisa smiled at Thoran like she was a sweet treat.

"Fine." Thoran replied. He began: "All right kids, listen carefully because I'm only saying this once…. It all started five years ago when a dark figure made his way through Triangle Woods. Triangle Woods is a forest in our world," she quickly summarized, answering all the unsaid questions that had popped onto Mike, Kirk and Liva's faces.

"Anyway, he ran till he came to a stone cave called Heavers Dean or the Prison of the Heavens. Inside, he went to a guard and gave him this badge." Mike looked down at the thing he had thought was a button that was identical to the one Thoran had in her hand.

"What does that mean?" he thought nervously, but allowed himself to listen to Thoran's story.

"He went to the red marked cell at the end of the hallway and went in. The prisoner inside was in prison because she had tried to steal the sole flames. The sole flames are a substance that were made in the forges of the outskirts before they were consumed by darkness. You see, the figure helped the prisoner escape. The name of the figure was Lord Devil, Lord Devil had hired the prisoner to steal the sole flames, but she had backed out. Lord Devil took the prisoner back to his castle and branded her arm as property of himself.

But the prisoner escaped. She has been on the run ever since…"

At that moment, Thoran rolled up her sleeve and showed the people in the room. There was a sloppy picture of a man in a 6-piece suit burned into her skin.

"Lord Devil," she finished.

Mike nearly gagged; it was the same man he had seen in the shack.

"That's all you had to say. I'm in," declared Liva.

"Tell us more about the prophecy," demanded Mike.

"Alright," Thoran looked at Thrisa and they both shrugged.

"Tell us more about the prophecy," Mike demanded.

"The prophecy is telling you what you have to do. The three t's are obviously me, Thrisa and…" she paused, took a deep breath and cautioned, "and Tothan my… brother. You must take the power of three and go through one of the last portals we have in our possession. Here's the badge." From the folds of her rags, Thoran drew out the badge. It was filled with grime and it was filthy, but Mike knew it would do.

Then, once you have gotten through the portal into the Stanchess, your task is simply to find the Hag of the Leaves. She is easy to find. And then she will give you passage to the Out-skirts where most evil dwells. Go to Lord Devil's castle, find the sole flames and return them to the Temple of the Flames.

Once the guardian of the flames has them back in her possession, she will take care of the rest. The gem is an old family heirloom of Lord Devil that confirmed Lord Devil's leadership of the whole world.

Oh, one more complication: You see, Hamlin, who is one of the team, has a… boyfriend." Thoran paused and her nose wrinkled, as if in disapproval. She only stopped for a moment and then barreled on: "And she will refuse to help you without him. He lives in a small town in Tran Tavern. Oh, and by the way, Hamlin was one of the workers that was there when one of the sole flames erupted. She absorbed its power, so just don't make her mad or insult her mom or she will literally blast you out of existence."

"Just don't make the girl mad. I can stand that--I'm in," smiled Kirk.

"Fine, but first tell me how to find Cand," Mike ordered.

"Cand has been kidnapped. The only way to rescue him is to go into the Outskirts and get him back."

Mike's world spun. "No!" he choked. His brother couldn't be a prisoner. It was just s-so unreal.

"One more thing--you need to watch out for the Dominions of Death," warned Thoran.

Kirk snorted. "Your world really needs to work on the names."

Thoran rounded on him, her eyes flashing: "The Dominions of Death are not a laughing matter. Large cloaked, there the henchman of Lord Devil, mark my words, you'll meet one of them on your journey. They are not to be fought with. I'm afraid Lord Devil has unleashed an army of them, and you'll do well to avoid them," prophesized Thoran darkly. She nodded at Thrisa. "Rember, Thrisa, watch out for them."

Mike felt a flood of relief. "You're coming with us!" he gasped.

Thrisa tossed her head. "You think I'd miss it!?"

"Here," Thoran dumped a few heavy satchels on Thrisa's back.

Liva and Kirk both had their backpacks, but Mike had left his somewhere in the woods. They didn't have time to retrieve it. Every second they wasted was a second that could be spent rescuing Cand.

"Remember, Thrisa, in the dungeons. Tothan, Cand and Flint, if he's alive. Do not, I repeat, do not come back for me if I get captured," breathed Thoran in Thrisa's ear. She looked quizzically at Thoran but didn't argue.

"Flint?!" exclaimed Mike. "He's alive?"

"We don't know," replied Thrisa.

Thoran grinded her teeth. Something was bothering her. "You have to go NOW!" she ordered.

Thrisa nodded. Her wings flapped up and down.

"Ready?" asked Mike.

Liva And Kirk nodded. Both of their gazes were fixed on the spot of air in front of them.

Thoran tossed the badge into the air.

The wind in the forest picked up. It swirled around and around ruffling Mike's hair. The wind swirled into a whirlpool and blue light began issuing from it.

Mike had to dig his feet into the ground so he wasn't blown away. He grasped hands with Liva and she did the same with Kirk.

Thrisa dug her talon's into the soft grass.

"We're coming, Cand," Mike thought fiercely as the portal took shape.

"NOW!" yelled Thrisa.

The group charged forward and the last thing Mike heard from Thoran was:

"Speed, Thrisa, that's what you're going to need." Then her voice filled with fear. "He's coming."

Mike didn't need to ask who was coming because he already knew. If Thoran didn't move fast enough, she was going to get captured by Lord Devil.

That was the last thought in Mike's head before the portal whisked him away.

Chapter Four
The Transformation

All Mike could see were flashes of blue light in a whirlpool of color. Occasionally, he would see a hand or a foot that belonged to Kirk or Liva, but when he reached out to grab them, they always twitched away from him.

One time he thought he saw Thrisa floating in midair in a seated position, but when he looked again, she was gone.

Without warning, all the light dropped away as soon as it had come.

Mike fell to the ground hard. If it wasn't for the hard landing, he would have thought he was dreaming for sure. Two more bumps and flashes of light and Kirk and Liva were sprawled next to him.

A third flash of light blazed through the world, and Thrisa appeared. Instead of falling to the ground, clumsily, like Mike, Liva and Kirk had done, she lifted her wings to their full extent and stopped her fall at the last second. She lifted her wings to the sky and swooped through the sky.

Mike shielded his eyes from the blaring sun and watched. Thrisa's wings caught on the sun like moonbeams. She seemed to dance in the light as if she was bathing in it. They stopped and stared in awe as Thrisa landed.

"Hi guys. Going through the portal never gets old, right? Let's see... we're right in between Blan Tavern and Transer Tavern," Thrisa chirped as cheerful as ever.

"What are the Blan Tavern and Transer Tavern?" Mike asked Thrisa.

"Oh dear, I almost forgot you weren't from this world... I'll tell you everything about it! Then you can study the map!" Thrisa thrust a small paper rolled up in a tight little scroll into Mike's hands.

He gingerly unrolled it and got a good look at it. It was a hand drawn map, but Mike recognized deep skill in the strokes. The map was made with a whole array of colors, but it seemed smudged somehow. Mike's eyes raked over the thin paper.

The whole continent was shaped roughly in the form of an arrow. In one corner of the continent, it was labeled 'The Stanchess' as if it was hushed away to the corner containing a collection of oddly shaped buildings all connected by a large web of rope or something stronger.

The buildings were labeled 'the Taverns' and there were seven in all. They read: The Smith Tavern, The Whole Tavern, The Hallie Tavern, The Denver Tavern, The Transer Tavern, Blan Tavern and Tran Tavern.

Parallel to the Taverns were two large shapes shaped in no particular shape. The larger of the two shapes was labeled 'Tefis Hold' and the smaller one had a label of 'Storage' on it.

All across the map, in two straight parallel lines, was a path that was labeled, 'the border line to the brink.'

Next to where the path started was a large building with crisscross patterns across it labeled: 'The Brink Base.' Outside the outline of the continent--but still fairly close to the Brink

Base-- was a large triangle flanked by several smaller triangles labeled: 'The Brink Base.'

On the very tip of The Stanchess was a small but large image of a tornado, all swirled up in black strokes as if someone had raked their pencil over the map. It was labeled: 'The Tornado Center'

Also outside the outline of The Stanchess, but still fairly close, were more scraggly lines that seemed to match The Tornado Center drawing. They were labeled: 'High Seas of The Tornados.'

Mike's eyes scanned back over to where the Taverns were. Straight on top of them was a large outline of a place called 'Space Time.' It was outlined in light purple simply because large objects that were brightly colored laid on top of the drawing.

Next to the Space Time fortress was a small triangle labeled: 'The Wrestlers Hold' it was completely surrounded by a path that was labeled 'The String Path.'

On the other side of the map, and farthest east that it seemed the Stanchess would go, was a small and not very majestic house that was labeled 'Tothan's hut.'

Mike stared at it in bewilderment for a moment. He specifically remembered Thrisa telling him that Tothan had been captured, and there was his hut, clear as day.

"It's always sad to look at it, isn't it? I mean, with Natone operating that house, it's cool and all, but Tothan was the best," Thrisa chirped from behind him, nearly making Mike jump out of his skin. Nodding absentmindedly, and not giving a response, he went back to studying every inch of the map.

Tothan's hut bordered a thin strip of red property that was labeled: 'Bracen's Property.' Directly above it, was a forest with oddly shaped trees, labeled: 'Triangle Woods.' In the depth of the woods was a large tent, surrounded by another couple of tents, all labeled: 'The Tonans Camp.'

Next to the woods was a large patch of land labeled: 'No Man's Land' and next to it was a another large patch of land with no label but a small drawing of what looked like a hourglass and was labeled in miniature writing: 'Table Turner'

Next to that was a tiny house that looked like it was surrounded by boulders, that was labeled 'Hevers Den' and in the very far corner and the edge of the Stanchess was a tiny triangle tucked into the folds of the land labeled 'Triangles Point'

Next to that on the very brim of the Stanchess was something that sent chills up Mike's spine. In jet black ink was a small but big stretch of land labeled 'the Outskirts,' and in the middle, was a red castle labeled 'Lord Devil's Castle.' Somewhere in there Cand was trapped, and Mike knew he had to get there in order to save his brother's life.

Mike wrenched his eyes from the frightening sight and instead placed them in the very center of the map where there was a large building labeled: The Temple of The Temple of The Soul Flames.' Mike gingerly rolled up the map and averted his attention back to Thrisa.

"So, what are the Taverns?" Liva asked.

"Er, there are seven taverns. Wait, I think I already told you that," Thrisa responded.

"Which one do we need to go to?" inquired Mike.

"Tran Tavern, but since we're closest to Blan Tavern, I think it's best we go there and find a room or something," answered Thrisa promptly.

"Yeah, we 'find a room.' What?" Liva said.

"Don't they have inns in your world?"

"Of course!"

"Then that's what I meant,"

"Fine."

A twig snapped somewhere. Thrisa leapt up in the air and raised her talons, trying to look threatening.

"I think it's only a chipmunk," Kirk remarked as he stifled a snort.

Thrisa looked extremely ruffled and became even more aggravated when a tiny chipmunk poked its head out of the bushes. Kirk looked like he was holding in laughter. Thrisa noticed it, too, and became incredibly annoyed.

"I'm sure YOU would be jumpy too if you knew that things were CHASING US!" Thrisa exclaimed grumpily.

"Chasing us?" echoed Kirk, a furrow in his brow appearing.

"Well, now you know," Thrisa responded with a hint of guilt in her tone.

"Who's chasing us?" demanded Liva.

Mike felt as if his world was tipping.

He was usually a good kid: he stayed to himself and tried not to get in trouble. Having someone--or something--chasing him and his friends was a whole new level.

"Bounty hunters," explained Thrisa, her voice low.

"Bounty hunters?" echoed Mike.

"Yeah, they were hired by Lord Devil to find us and bring them to him," Thrisa shuddered. "They could be anything, any species. They could be Dominons of Death. They could be vipers…I don't know,"

"That is… incredibly unnerving," noted Kirk.

"That's why we should hurry," agreed Thrisa. "Just keep your head down and don't talk to anybody."

"But, Thrisa, this place is so big! Even if we *do* avoid the bounty hunters after us, how are we going to find the Hag of Leaves in a place like this? You told us that she lived in Tothan's old house, but what if she moved? What if she isn't there anymore? What if we c-can't f-find Cand i-in time??" Mike ranted, his voice cracking and his face falling.

Thrisa's cheerful demeanor seemed to fade away. Her head drooped and she looked so sad. Mike almost wanted to take back his words. They seemed to cut into Thrisa like small knives.

"I don't know, I don't know," admitted Thrisa heavily.

***

Thrisa had been able to get a room in Blan Tavern without attracting too much attention or using much of the money Thoran gave them.

Mike examined one of the copper coins Thrisa had used to pay the inn. "This coin... it's so different from ours. How much is it worth?" Mike asked Thrisa.

"That's a wimble. What do you mean how much is it worth? Store folk simply say like, five wimbles, that's it," replied Thrisa. "Oh, and one more thing… when we enter the inn, try not to stare at anything," Thrisa added sheepishly.

"Oh, that will be easy!" Liva exclaimed. After she had said that, she shot a wink to Mike.

"Ok, onward!" Thrisa exclaimed. She came down from the spot in midair where she was floating and came to rest on Mike's shoulder.

Mike immediately felt his shoulder groan in protest under Thrisa's weight. Mike pushed open the brown inn door in front of him and it took his breath away.

Inside the inn it looked like a scene from an alien movie. There was a bar pushed to the side and a spiral staircase leading up to the rooms, probably. There was a band playing in the middle of the room.

But it was not people but other creatures in the room. There was a pink blob with no arms or legs. When a waiter placed a glass of green liquid in front of him, he sucked it up and grew larger. There were several more of these blobs in the room. There was also a man-sized stick but with tentacles. The only other species in the room were things that looked exactly like humans, but Mike knew they couldn't be.

"Try not to attract attention. Let's go to the room so we can give you some power," Thrisa hissed in Mike's ear and beckoned for Kirk and Liva to follow. Liva kept tripping and nearly falling over her own feet because she was staring (despite Thrisa's protests) at her surroundings. Kirk was walking with his head down not looking at anything but his own shoes.

Finally, they reached the stairs and Mike slammed the door to their room.

"Alright, let's give you some power!" Thrisa purred happily, "All you have to do is pick a power. You can be a fighter, a magick, or a thief. The fighter can fight really well and even get this really cool sword! The magick is like a wizard in your world. Once the magick is in your veins, you will understand. And the thief can pick locks, has a bunch of cool gadgets and can turn invisible. So, you have to pick one!" Thrisa explained to them.

"We get superpowers!? Cool! I'll take the magick!"

"I'll be the thief," Kirk mumbled.

"I'll be the… fighter," Mike decided.

"Ok, this might feel a bit weird. I am transferring the power into you." Thrisa admitted apologetically. Thrisa opened the capsule that contained the power. The power shot towards Mike, Kirk and Liva.

The power seemed to go through Mike. He felt himself changing, his senses getting stronger. He also realized that in his hand he held a bronze sword that was crackling with electricity, and he was wearing armor.

He saw Kirk and Liva changing too. Liva's clothes changed into a long flowing cloak and her hands sparkled with electricity like Mile's sword had. Kirk was flickering in between seeing him and not seeing him. His clothes had changed too. Instead of T-shirt and jeans, he wore a small cloak that went down to his knees and tight red pants with a shirt that was covered by his cloak. A belt filled with gadgets completed his appearance. Mike felt stronger than he had ever had.

"You know we should probably leave about right now," Thrisa remarked nervously.

"Why? We just got here," asked Mike who was looking forward to sinking into the bed.

"Because I might have seen a few bounty hunters and the barman ponting at us, so we should go!" Thrisa explained, talking more rapidly by the second.

A loud tinkering sound filled the room. "Get down!" Thrisa shouted just as the wall behind them was blown to pieces.

Mike covered his head with his hands and turned around to see who had caused the damage.

"Mike! I have our baggage--meet me outside. This one is up to you! Ok? I will see you soon," hissed Thrisa in Mike's ear. And with that she flew out the open window.

He twisted around to see who had caused the blast. Standing in the hole they had made were undoubtedly bounty hunters. They both had guns in their hands. One shouted at the chandelier that was hanging over his head, plunging the room into darkness.

Mike cried out in pain as part of the chandelier crashed down on his legs. Mike could hardly think with the chandelier on his legs but then he heard the bounty hunter say, "Find them, capture the grandson and gorgalin, kill the other two."

Rage coursed through Mike. He forced the chandelier off his legs and ran at the bounty hunters.

"There! Set the gun on him!" shouted one bounty hunter to another.

Mike lept on the first one and kicked him in the head. The bounty hunter turned and threw him over his head onto the ground. Mike kicked up as hard as he could. Judging by the grunt, he knew his foot had met its mark. The first bounty hunter crumpled to the ground. All Mike's senses seemed more alert than they had ever had.

Mike could tell that the second bounty hunter was right behind him wielding a knife. Mike turned and punched the bounty hunter in the jaw. He reached to do it again, but he wasn't quick enough. The bounty hunter reached down and stabbed him in the arm. Mike screamed in agony and fell to the ground. The pain from the chandelier slowly came back to him.

The bounty hunter slowly advanced upon him. The bounty hunter tossed the bloody dagger aside and picked up Mike's sword that he had dropped when he had fallen to the ground.

Mike groaned and clutched his arm as the bounty hunter rasped, "Yea' know Devil said at' bring my grandson bac' alive but me reall' don't see the difference, so he'll have to settle for died." He raised the sword and Mike braced himself.

"But, you see, I see a big difference," said a voice out of nowhere. Several ropes came out of thin air and bound the bounty hunter.

"Liva!" Mike shouted but winced when he tried to move his arm.

"Mike, let me look at that." She looked at him and he smiled.

Liva's eyes glowed green and she said, "Thomanso Donan."

"When did you learn to do that? Your powers are so much cooler than mine!" Mike said in awe he stared down at his newly healed arm.

Liva shrugged. "I guess since I saw you in danger, my powers activated kinda like yours, you know?"

"Where's Kirk?" asked Mike.

"Oh, I think he's picking the bounty hunters' pockets."

"Hi, guys. That was really cool when you fought those guys, Mike."

"Thanks, I think we should be more careful next time," decided Mike.

"Agreed," both Kirk and Liva said as the three friends stepped out of the hole the bounty hunters had made.

Chapter Five
Life of Crime

Mike, Kirk and Liva quickly hurried out of the inn and met Thrisa outside.

"Hiii, boy, am I glad to see you! What happened there? Tell me everything!" insisted Thrisa.

Mike and Kirk told Thrisa everything that had happened inside the inn. "And then he said…" Mike trailed off. He frowned. "There's something I don't understand that the bounty hunter said: 'Devil said bring my grandson back alive.' But who is his grandson?" asked Mike.

Thrisa sighed heavily, "I thought Thoran would have told you… since she is the mother of Lord Devil and the wife of your great grandfather. Mike... Lord Devil is your… your grandfather."

The world spun around Mike like a torrent of water lashing at him. He clutched his head and tried to think.

"No, impossible...Mother said he had died at sea! And Thoran can't be my great

grandmother. She is about the same age as my mother!" Mike thought in distress.

"Eternal youth," whispered Thrisa. Mike looked at her and she explained, "Thoran has eternal youth. The earrings she wears have eternal youth in them. Ever since your great grandfather died, it broke her heart." Thrisa confessed.

"But that's impossible--what kind of grandfather kidnaps his own grandson!" Mike exclaimed.

"Just get some sleep. We can camp close to Tran Taverns' gates and we'll get there in the morning. I'll make a fire.

***

Mike sat and stared at the stars.

"The stars are so different than in our world." Mike sighed and began again, "Why didn't Thoran tell me, Thrisa? When she knocked me out, she could have told me," Mike said in a sad tone.

"She would have… but Lord Devil came first--that's why we had two leave so fast."

"It's just that… I don't know what I'm doing! We just got attacked by a bunch of random people!" Mike exploded, "Tell me the truth, Thrisa. What's going on here! No more shortcuts or lies!"

"Fine! You want to know? I will tell you everything, but hear this, it is not what it seems: Once there was a young boy that lived in the countryside with his mother and father. All was well till the boy's father grew very sick and died the very next day. The boy went on a rampage around the country despite his mother's protest. He never felt the same way for his mother as he had felt for his father.

The little boy grew into a sorrowful young man. He soon began to be known as Lord Devil.

One day Lord Devil came across a badge on the floor of his room. It opened up a portal and he went through, dragging his mother with him. Lord Devil locked up his mother in his castle that he had built for himself.

Several years later, Lord Devil was determined to hatch a powerful heir that he could control. Soon after, he married a powerful and vain woman. She bore two daughters. One was a very powerful person and had extraordinary powers. The other was defective and had none. In disgust, Lord Devil threw away the baby into his home world. Lord Devil concealed his wife and powerful child in a cave for them to wait for his call.

But the night Lord Devil was out, his mother escaped. Lord Devil tracked her down and said that he would spare her life if his mother brought him the Soul Flames. With the Soul Flames power, he could bring his father back from the dead, which would probably destroy the world.

Lord Devil grew more and more powerful over time and now has your brother as leverage and the Soul Flames. The only good thing is that the Soul Flames only activate in the brightest night which is in five days--so we really need to go fast."

"Are you telling me that Thoran was the mother in the story and that Lord Devil's off-spring was my mother!?" Mike exclaimed. "But that wouldn't make sense! Mom has parents. I've seen them!"

"Your mother has adopted parents. They just never told her," Thrisa said gently. A twig snapped in the distance.

"Shhh, they will hear you!" said an angry voice.

Mike sighed, "Liv, Kirk, you can come out!" he called into the bushes.

"Oh, good. I was getting really antsy hiding in the bushes! Oh, and by the way, this was definitely Kirk's idea," Liva said as she crawled out of the bushes.

"It wasn't my idea--you made that up!" Kirk exclaimed.

"Anyway, how much did you hear?" asked Thrisa, pushing away Liva and Kirk's scandal as if it wasn't important to her.

"Oh, pretty much all of it, since Kirk is a thief. He is invisible right now."

"I was experimenting with my powers and found this cool feature where no one can hear you. But then Mr. Loud Face snapped a twig."

"Does that mean Mike has cool powers?!" Liva smiled and glared at the empty air.

"Alright, I am here," a small voice peeped. With a pop, Kirk appeared. "That's really hard to process. I am glad I don't have any creepy ties in this world," Kirk said happily as he rested a comforting hand on Mike's shoulder.

"Your mother dated Lord Devil when he lived in your world." Thrisa said with a snicker.

"Noo! Why did you have to tell me that?" Kirk asked.

"Yes, Liva, Mike will have the power of the Outskirts. The next full moon he will be at his prime--that's why Lord Devil has sent about every bounty hunter there is after you. Plus, with a bounty on your head, it's going to be hard to travel," Thrisa replied.

"What about Flint and Tothan? What happened to them?" Mike asked Thrisa.

"Tothan is being held prisoner at Lord Devil's castle (another person to rescue). And Flint... well... Flint is dead. He tried to resist, but Lord Devil killed him," Thrisa said sadly.

Flint's death was what made everything seem so real to Mike that people were dying. "And Eva and her brother?" Mike asked Thrisa again.

Thrisa smirked. "Eva, right? Well, that's her pen name. Her real name is Hamlin, daughter of the Hag of Leaves, Natone. And her brother was also killed by Lord Devil.

"Is that why her eyes were red? The soul flame inside her?" Kirk asked curiously.

"That's why Thoran was sad when she told me that Cand had been kidnapped. I wonder what Cand is doing right now. I hope he isn't alone. And that Lord Devil is feeding him alright. He's been prisoner for a day now," Mike thought sadly.

"That's why we have to keep moving in the morning," Thrisa was telling Kirk and Liva.

"Another thing you should know is that when Lord Devil uses the power of the flames, he will use your world as an anchor. And I am afraid your world isn't meant to survive," Thrisa finished gravely.

Chapter Six
An Unexpected Death

"Why would Lord Devil do that just to bring back his father? He must care about Earth because he lived there, too," Kirk said, turning to Thrisa in the process.

"Lord Devil has been driven mad with grief. He will destroy anything or anyone just to get his father back," Thrisa replied.

"Why won't Earth survive when Lord Devil tries to bring his father back?" asked Mike.

"Lord Devil will use the Soul Flames like a time machine, except he won't go back in time himself. He will order the Soul Flames to pluck his father out of time itself. Lord Devil needs all Earth's resources to make it work.

Once Lord Devil has gotten his father back, the passageway will become unstable. In order to stay connected, the Soul Flames will destroy Earth," Thrisa explained.

"We need to get Hamlin's boyfriend and get to Lord Devil before he destroys Earth!" exclaimed Kirk.

"Right! Grab something to eat and go to bed. We leave at dawn tomorrow," Thrisa called as Kirk, Liva and Mike disappeared into the bushes to find a warm spot in the chilly air.

"Mike, wait!" Thrisa called after Mike.

"What?"

"I have news on your brother from Thoran."

"Alright," he said, "I'm listening."

"Thoran believes that Lord Devil means to sacrifice your brother to the Soul Flames," Thrisa grimaced. "Go to bed now, Mike. I will see you in the morning."

Mike turned without another word, but before he disappeared into the thrush, he asked Thrisa, "The legend of Spook Woods says that Ev--Hamlin has a brother. Who is he?"

Thrisa smiled, "Indeed Hamlin has a brother. Not long after Hamlin was born, Natone gave birth to another. Butttttt he is dead now, so no need to worry about him,"

Mike nodded satisfied, disappearing into the thrush.

***

"Are you going to tell me what she wanted with you?" asked Liva when Mike got to a clearing.

"No, I don't think I will," replied Mike.

Liva nudged his shoulder affectionately.

"Monster," mumbled Kirk. Mike and Liva both laughed, laid down, and stared up at the stars.

***

Thrisa woke them up by sitting on them one at a time.

"Ahh! Get off baby hippo!" screamed Kirk. Thrisa giggled, moving to Kirk's face to smother the screams.

Kirk's shouts jolted Mike awake. At first he thought he was safe in bed at home and this had all been a crazy dream with Cand sleeping next to him. All the events of the past day came rushing back to him: Thrisa, Cand, Thoran, his ties to the Stanchess. Cand...

"Give us Devil's grandson or face the consequences," hissed a raspy voice. Before he knew it, his hands were tied behind his back and he was being dragged roughly to his feet.

"Quit struggling, you, or your friend dies." Mike saw a knife be raised to Kirk's neck...

"No!" protested Mike and Liva together.

Liva struggled even more.

Mike's captor shoved him to the ground. He tried to get up, but he put a foot on his chest.

Mike heard a swish of a knife. Kirk crumpled to the ground and didn't get up again. Mike was blinded with grief. He couldn't see or think his best friend was dead.

A bright flash showed the arrival of Thrisa. She was accompanied by a woman Mike didn't know. The woman that accompanied Thrisa was a beautiful middle-aged woman, (or looked like a woman, Mike was not sure what she was yet.) She had auburn hair tied in a long braid, was dressed in a flowing cloak and had pale skin.

Thrisa flashed her talons and beat her wings, preparing to fight.

"You're making a grave mistake, woman. You too, Gorgalina. There is a reason we killed your kind."

"Capture the Gorgalina. Devil will want to question it," the first voice said to the other.

"No one calls me 'it'!" shrieked Thrisa, leaping into something Mike could not see.

The woman's eyes began to glow. Strong blasts shot out of her as she began to fight alongside Thrisa.

Mike sucked in his breath as he realized who this woman was: she was Hamlin, daughter of the Hag of Leaves. The prophecy was coming true.

Despite Kirk's death that was drilling holes in his heart, he couldn't help but stare in awe at Hamlin fighting his captor. Mike fought against the ropes that bound him and eventually broke free. Mike ran to Liva's side (the voice that had held her was busy fighting Thrisa.) They stumbled over to Kirk's body and collapsed on the ground next to it.

Mike didn't know how to fight something he couldn't see, so he just rested his head on Kirk's body and watched the battle progress. Hamlin was being driven to the ground by invisible hands.

"Say goodbye to the world, woman," rasped an invisible voice. A knife appeared.

"Not yet," panted Hamlin. "Ackooooooo," she called.

"You call that a lifesaver!" chortled the voice.

"Not that, this," she retorted.

Suddenly, a boy about as old as Hamlin rammed into the invisible voice.

"Hamlin!" he shouted.

Hamlin and the boy came into a giant embrace. "I missed you so much! Where have you be--" The boy was cut short and fell to the ground with a knife in his back.

Chapter Seven
The Truth

Cand was a prisoner, Devil was his grandfather, Flint was dead, Hamlin's boyfriend was dead, Tothan was a prisoner, Earth was halfway doomed... Worst of all, Kirk, his best friend, was dead and it was his fault. (Perhaps Cand's imprisonment was tied with Kirk's death.)

These thoughts circled around in his head for the remainder of the fight. Before long, all the invisible voices were defeated.

Hamlin was on the ground weeping for her fallen friend. Thrisa crouched over Hamlin, murmuring comforting words.

"Thank you, you saved our lives," Mike thanked Thrisa and Hamlin. Mike felt a sudden rush of sadness that swept through him like a storm.

"Except Kirk, some help she did with that. Wonder if she would feel so high and mighty if her *best friend had died,"* Mike thought bitterly. But even as he thought it, his heart didn't believe it.

"No, at least not every one," Hamlin remarked as bitterly as Mike.

Thrisa frowned at Mike. Her brow furrowed. He realized she had probably read his mind and discovered his traitorous thoughts.

"Sorry," he mouthed to her.

Mike let the tears that were brimming in his eyes fall onto Kirk's body.

"I am so sorry about your friend. I could not save him," Hamlin told Mike. When Mike looked up, surprised, Hamlin continued: "Your friend was fated to fall…" Mike looked into her eyes, and a vision surfaced.

He saw a brightly lit room: there was a blob (that looked exactly like the one Mike had seen in the inn), a stick man, a marble statue of a woman, and a hooded creature.

"We must decide now!" said the blob.

"We do not know if this person is a threat or an ally!" retorted the stick man.

"Is that what they call them? People?" asked the marble statue.

"It sure looks like you!" added the marble statue, nodding at the hooded figure.

"There are plenty of species that look like these humans! We lastrongs are nothing like them!" snarled the hooded figure.

"Stop this, all of you!" shouted the stick man. "None of us have known that humans existed till yesterday!"

"Oh, don't be stupid! All of us have seen this human up close before!" shouted the blob.

"I always assumed he was a polynom," brooded the hooded figure.

"Wait! I think I found something!" exclaimed the marble statue.

A stormy picture of Kirk flooded onto the table they were sitting at.

"He is a thief. Their blood will be able to hold on the little Devil a bit longer till we get a permanent solution!" The marble statue reported.

"Pity we have to end his life so soon!" the blob said roughly.

"We have no choice! The fate of the Stanchess is in our hands!" protested the stick man. The room fell silent. "End his life. Give him a hero's death," the stick man said gravely. "Nashena, guard the Soul Flames until the thief's blood runs out!" ordered the stick man.

A snake slithered into the room and hissed: "Yesssss masssssssster. I will guard them with my life."

A strong metal door opened with a thud, revealing seven flames burning brightly in the piths.

"Bad move to open the door," said a voice.

"Daniel!" the hooded figure said, jumping to his feet.

"They call me Lord Devil now!" Lord Devil said coolly.

"To me, you are still little Daniel," replied the hooded figure as he lowered his hood.

"Uncle Tothan? It's really you…" Lord Devil sputtered for a moment. Fear flickered across his face, but he quickly shoved it down again. "My mother, you have her, don't you?" asked Lord Devil.

"Yes, I do. I had to leave earth. I got a bad reputation ever since you killed Eva's brother!"

"Ah, yes, mother is still pretending to be a polymotho?" asked Lord Devil.

"Yes, please Daniel, stop this. You will not be able to bring back your father," pleaded Tothan.

Anger flitted through Lord Devil's face. He reached towards Tothan's outstretched hand and cut it off with a knife.

"By the way, he lied about being lastrong! He is human!" Lord Devil cried and threw Tothan at their feet.

In three quick movements, Lord Devil threw knives at the stick man, the statue and the blob. All daggers hit their mark.

Lord Devil then advanced upon the Soul Flames. Nashena hissed and lunged at him, but Lord Devil fought with the strength of ten snakes and she was quickly overpowered.

Lord Devil shoved the snake aside and reached for the Flames. Tothan scrambled forward and seized Lord Devil with his good hand. Lord Devil reached the Soul Flames, scooped them up, and fired them at the sky causing the roof to cave in. Lord Devil disappeared in a flash of blue light dragging Tothan with him.

The snake lunged at Lord Devil, but it was too late. Lord Devil and Tothan were gone, and he had the Soul Flames.

Chapter Eight
The Warning

The vision of the room broke away as quickly as it had come. Mike stumbled away from Hamlin clutching his head.

"Mike!" gasped Liva. "Are you all right?"

"Yes, I am fine," he replied.

Mike turned to Hamlin and demanded, "What was that!"

"A vision of the truth," replied Hamlin.

"Are you telling me what happened the night Lord Devil took the Soul Flames?" asked Mike.

"Yes," replied Hamlin. "That is what Tothan and Thoran are trying to hide from you. They alone have the power to conceal Lord Devil, but a great power comes with great responsibility. Not even Thrisa knows this since they are related to Lord Devil. Much like you at foul moon, all of you will have great power. But power demands sacrifices; one will not survive the defeat of Lord Devil. Thoran plans to sacrifice herself to defeat Lord Devil," finished Hamlin.

The prophesied death of Thoran was just too much for Mike. He ran into the bushes and didn't return for some time. Mike wiped his nose on the corner of his sleeve. His instinct told him that a life form was approaching. Mike turned in alarm, scared that more of the invisible voices had caught up with him.

"Your skills need work. You should know that. It's not a Dominion of Death. It's just me, Mike."

Mike breathed a sigh of relief when he recognized Thrisa's voice. "I know you are trying to cheer me up, but it won't work," Mike called to Thrisa. He looked behind him and immediately regretted his words.

Thrisa was hunched over, her wings wrapped around her lion body. She was shivering violently (probably from the shock of hearing that one of her closest friends was planning to sacrifice herself to stop her own son.)

"I might never know how you feel…" Thrisa hesitated. He realized she was thinking of

Thoran and her untimely death. "But let me do something about it. Please, we need to finish what we started! By stopping Lord Devil you would have avenged Kirk's death. Hamlin is preparing to fly to her mother's land. It will take the remainder of the morning but it is the quickest way…"

***

Ten minutes later Thrisa had gathered all their belongings. Liva was refusing to leave without giving Kirk a proper funeral.

"Yeah," agreed Mike.

"Alright, you do what you need to do." Mike got the feeling that Thrisa's tone would have been more teasing if their best friend hadn't just died.

Mike helped Liva dig a small trench using Liva's magic. Liva even coaxed a seed hidden deep inside the earth out. It bloomed out as a small green plant with a tiny blossom.

Tears littered the ground from Mike and Liva. His heart felt like a canal, as if it had been split open. They laid him to rest and Mike could hardly choke out a few words before they buried him.

"One more thing," Mike added as he wiped his eyes on his sleeve. "How were those things there? How could I feel them but not see them?" he demanded.

"The Dominions of Death are dark creatures. They live in secrecy, can turn invisible, and melt into the darkness like a mere shadow." Thrisa explained in a soft but foreboding voice.

"Once you have defeated them, they are forced to reveal themselves," Hamlin added. "Watch."

Mike didn't know what he was watching, so he just looked at Hamlin. "Sometimes, if you can find their bodies and touch them, they will be forced to reveal themselves," Hamlin clarified. She groped around for a moment and finally she seemed to have found something.

Mike took a tentative step back as ten or so bodies were flung into existence. They were cloaked, so their faces were obscured. Even though they were dead, Mike could sense the pure evil radiating from them.

"But, how do you know if they are not right behind you?" asked Liva. Her face was paler than usual.

"You do not," replied Hamlin simply.

Mike suppressed a shudder with difficulty.

"That's why Lord Devil hired them; they make great henchmen. Mike, you can ride with me, and Liva can ride with Hamlin," instructed Thrisa.

"How am I going to ride with Hamlin? She's not big enough," Liva inquired, speaking for the first time since Kirk's funeral. Her voice was flat and her face shined with tears but she looked so curious. Mike felt his heart inflate a bit with hope. She wasn't too succumbed by their loss to wonder. Maybe they could overcome this loss.

"Mike is too big for me too," replied Thrisa simply. Thrisa looked at Hamlin expectantly.

Hamlin looked uncomfortable but raised her hand. Flame gushed out of it, creating a raft of flames. Liva gingerly prodded the raft but sat down all the same.

Mike turned back to the bodies. He wanted to see them one more time before he left. Mike crouched down beside one of the Dominions of Death's bodies.

"Beware, a mother and wife you cannot trust," the body rasped. Mike stumbled away in shock.

"Mike, are you coming?" asked Thrisa. "Yes, yes," replied Mike. He stumbled away and fell onto Thrisa's back. Mike looked back again at the Dominions of Death's body. Had it just given him a prophecy?

Chapter Nine
The Wrestlers

Mike, Thrisa, Hamlin, and Liva were flying over the Stanchess in the direction of Tothan's hut. Mike was holding the map aloft, trying to see where they were going, when Thrisa turned around and nipped the map away in her mouth.

"You won't be needing that!" she exclaimed and dropped it down into the land below. When Mike tried to protest, she added, "I know it all by heart, anyway."

"We are approaching Wrestlers Hold now, home of the Wrestlers," Hamlin called out to Thrisa and Mike.

"Next time, I'm asking Liva for a ride. She is much nicer than you!" Thrisa said grumpily.

Mike couldn't help but think about the warning that the Dominion of Death had issued. "He couldn't be talking about Thoran, could he? Wife to my great grandfather and mother to Lord Devil?" he thought nervously, but quickly pushed that thought away.

"We should stop at Wrestlers Hold. It is the only place for miles," Hamlin confirmed.

"We need to get a champ," replied Thrisa.

"What is a champ?" asked Liva.

"The Wrestlers make whoever comes into their territory wrestle to the death, so one thing from each group is the champ. If the champ loses, then the wrestlers have permission to kill all the travelers. But if the champ wins, then they get a royal welcome," explained Hamlin.

"I vote Mike for champ!" declared Liva.

"It will be a good idea," mused Hamlin.

"Who do I have to defeat?" asked Mike, looking from Thrisa to Hamlin to Liva.

"That is the choice of the king and his wife," replied Hamlin.

"Alright, I'll be champ," sighed Mike.

***

"We have arrived!" cried Hamlin. Mike saw a gigantic fortress looming out at them. Before he knew it, Thrisa was diving down in a nose dive and landing next to the big double doors. Hamlin landed beside them with Liva on the raft.

"Since the Wrestler tribe got a small portion of the land, they are a bit unruly." explained Hamlin.

Thrisa knocked lightly on the double doors.

"Who goes there?" asked a voice inside the door.

"Travelers! Seeking shelter!" replied Hamlin.

The door swung open. "Travelers! Come in, come in, King Rupert has an opponent for you!" said a grizzly butler.

Mike stepped into the room and immediately wanted to get out. The room was large with a platform in the middle and dozens of bars all around. On the other side of the room were two thrones with a King on one and a Queen on the other. Multiple staircases wound up to the ceiling and beyond. Several hundreds of Wrestlers milled around the room, drinking mead. The Wrestlers had two fangs hanging out of their mouth and were the size of a full grown man.

When Hamlin, Thrisa, Mike, Liva and the butler entered the room, all conversation ended abruptly. One Wrestler stopped moving with his fork halfway to his mouth.

The King jumped to his feet and said, in a booming voice, "Travelers! Welcome! I have an opponent ready for you!"

"Right to the point," muttered Mike to Liva.

Thrisa gave Mike a slight push in the direction of the ring.

"The rules are simple: Fight to the death, you may kill or yield, dirty tricks are expected, no weapons... if yo-" The king was cut off abruptly by the Queen who said, "They know the rules, dear. Now get to the point. I want to see this." The king nodded and signaled for a burly Wrestler to come to the ring.

Mike scrambled up and faced his opponent. The bulky Wrestler grinned down at him. Another small wiry Wrestler clambered up onto the ring and produced a rope that crackled with electricity out of his bag. The wiry Wrestler thrashed Mike and the bulky Wrestler together. Once the wiry Wrestler was done, he scurried back out of the ring.

Mike searched the crowd for his friends. He found them: Hamlin nodded at him, Thrisa nodded encouragingly and Liva gave him the thumbs up.

"...Get ready, face your opponent, anddddd... attack!" the King was saying.

Before Mike had time to turn around, he received a stunning blow to his stomach. He doubled over and staggered back. The rope that bound Mike and the Wrestler together crackled and turned purple. It shocked Mike and dragged him back to face his opponent.

The Wrestler was too busy laughing and cheering at the crowd to notice his opponent getting up. Mike staggered at him and tried to swipe at his legs to unbalance him.

The Wrestler was too quick for Mike. He swooped down on him and put a foot on his chest. Pain coursed through Mike as he felt his ribs break. Mike woefully wished for his sword that he had left with Thrisa.

The Wrestler smiled evilly at him and drew a sword from his belt. The Wrestler loomed over him, sword drawn. "No weapons," mumbled Mike. The wrestler paid no mind to breaking his King's rules. Mike desperately looked to the King for support, but the King was too busy chatting with his Queen to notice.

The Wrestler raised his sword, preparing to strike, fury burning deep inside Mike. he had come so far, suffered so much pain, lost his brother and best friend to be defeated by a bully! New found strength burned in Mike and he sprang from the ground and faced his opponent.

The Wrestler, taken by surprise, tried to swing his sword but Mike was too fast. Mike pounded on the Wrestlers face till he fell to the ground dead.

"Magnifancint!" cried the King. "Now, I have the perfect job for you! You will stay here for all eternity! And fight!"

"Uh… sir… I'm not sure I can do it…" stammered Mike.

"Why ever not?" asked the King

"I just… have…. Things to do?" Mike replied, the whole room gasped in shock that the stranger had refused their King.

"In that case, attack!" cried the King. Dozens of Wrestlers came pouring into the ring. Mike and his friends outside the ring were soon surrounded.

Chapter Ten
The Escape

Mike tossed Wrestlers out of his way as he struggled to meet his friends in the middle of the room.

The Wrestler King fell back into his throne with a satisfied sigh, now that his 'guests' were being taken care of. The Wrestler Queen had taken out a sort of knitting and was watching the battle with interest.

"I killed that guy! I killed him!" was all Mike could think as he fought his way towards Thrisa, Hamlin and Liva. Mike had lost control when the bulky Wrestler had knocked him down…Lord Devil! He had felt as his grandfather had acted!

Out of his corner of his eye, Mike saw Thrisa lift up into the air. Hamlin quickly followed, flames blasted out of Hamlin's hands, making her hair fall straight down on her back, the usual wave in it gone. (Mike thought she looked rather pretty.)

Thrisa swooped down, slashing Wrestlers with her claws. Liva was in the thick of the fighting dodging swords and akses, making vines grow out of the ground and twisting around Wrestlers' feet. Hamlin was blasting Wrestler after Wrestler with flames from her spot in the sky.

"They seem not to care about you," hissed a voice in his ear.

"Dominions of Death!" Mike thought fearfully. They had found him!

"Come on, Mike!" cried Thrisa.

"Until we meet again little hero," spat the Dominion of Death. The presence Mike had felt when the Dominion of Death was so close faded into nothing.

Mike ran after Thrisa towards the door. Hamlin blasted the door open. Mike hurried forward. Suddenly, a hand reached out and grabbed him by the scruff of the neck. The Wrestler King was holding him aloft for all of his subjects to see.

"This, Wrestlers, is the tyrant who refused me!" cried the King. At this the Wrestlers roared and began pelting Mike with any spare things.

"Go get your little friend," spat the King to Thrisa, Hamlin and Liva. (All of them were in the air. Liva was on Thrisa's back.) None of Mike's friends moved. They stared down at the king, their faces stony. Mike saw a flicker of fear flash through Liva's face.

The King threw Mike on the ground.

Hamlin let out a war cry and dived. She circled once around Mike and conjured thick ropes that wound and wriggled until they formed a kind of net. Hamlin shoved Mike inside the net and took off into the air with the net clasped tightly in her hands.

"I'll get you! Daughter of the Hag of Leaves! Archers!" barked The King. Several Wrestlers readied bows... but it was too late. Mike, Thrisa, Hamlin and Liva were soaring out the door into open skies.

Chapter Eleven
The Arrival

Mike squirmed into a better position in the net as they soared over the ruins of the temple of the Soul Flames.

"Hamlin...uh... thanks for going back for me back there," Mike thanked. There was a pause.

"Mike, you are my friend... I would have done the same for the others," Hamlin replied.

"Thrisa didn't do anything; Liva didn't do anything," Mike added softly.

Hamlin frowned. "I can not watch someone die while I can save them," Hamlin replied simply.

"Oh... well I was just wondering... I've got a question for you. I've been meaning to say this for a while now. What are you?" asked Mike.

"Pardon?" Hamlin said, taken aback.

"What's the species you and your mom are?" Mike continued.

"Oh! Oh... you mean that! My mom is descended from a long line of sorcerers. We sorcerers do not believe in marriage. My mother became an outcast ever since… she married my father, that is why I never knew him." Hamlin explained. For a moment, Mike could see emotion across Hamlin's face.

"I'm sorry," Mike said softly.

"It does not matter. How can you miss someone you never met?" asked Hamlin briskly. "It is just… that sometimes I am mad at him for abandoning us even though he had no choice."

"I felt the same way after my brother was captured. I was mad at him for sneaking away, but worried sick for him anyway," Mike confessed.

"I am sorry for your brother, Mike," Hamlin said. And at that moment they both shared a smile.

"Oy! Love birds! We're approaching the brink base, so if I were you, I would fly higher!" called Thrisa. Hamlin blushed crimson at this comment and jerked the net higher. Mike settled down in the net and listened to the sound of the wind around him.

"This net feels awkward... I wonder if Dominions of Death can fly?... Hamlin seems so nice... I hardly knew her and she risked her life for me!.. Hamlin has such a tragic backstory... I wonder what Kirk would think of this... I wonder what Cand, Thoran and Tothan are doing right now? Rotting in a dungeon I s'pose... Oh, yeah! I have to tell the others about the encounter with the Dominion of Death!" Mike's string of thoughts ended abruptly when he remembered the Dominion of Death. He was about to call to the others when a giant figure of rocks loomed out of the mist.

"The Brink Base," breathed Thrisa.

They floated above the base for a while before the fortress disappeared into the mist. They spent the rest of the trip in silence. Eventually, a hard path came into view followed by a crumpling cave.

"Hamy," sang a voice.

"Mother!" cried Hamlin.

Hamlin smiled happily as Thrisa and Hamlin touched down on the ground. They had reached the home of the Hag of Leaves.

Chapter Twelve
The Hag of Leaves

Hamlin dropped Mike's net approximately twenty feet from the ground.

"Ahhhhh!" he shrieked as he plummeted down to the earth below. Thrisa swooped and caught him before he hit the ground.

Mike scrambled out of the net. "Thank you," he told Thrisa as she landed beside him somewhat breathlessly.

After he finished thanking her, he took in his surroundings. They were in a deep crater. In the very middle, there was a small hut and a garden surrounding it. A few trees dotted the landscape. Other than that, all Mike could see was dirt and rock for miles around.

A small woman (or sorcerer) was hobbling towards them. Mike knew immediately that this woman was the Hag of Leaves, Natone. Natone was short but gave off a powerful aura. She had the same auburn hair as her daughter. Natone's piercing green eyes were enough to scare the bravest person away.

Hamlin ran at her mother and they embraced. Mike, Liva and Thrisa were more hesitant to approach.

"Mother, this is Mike, Liva and the Gorgelina," introduced Hamlin.

"Thrisa," corrected Thrisa.

"Thrisa," repeated Hamlin.

"Pleasure, please come in for tea and bread," invited Natone as she led them into her house.

***

After they were safely inside the hut, Mike was able to take in the inside of Natone's hut and her appearance. Mike noticed a silver wedding ring on Natone's finger.

"That's odd… shouldn't she have hid or destroyed her ring after she had Hamlin?" Mike thought curiously.

Natone caught Mike staring at her ring and quickly shoved the hem of her sleeve to cover it up. She smiled sweetly at Mike, and he looked up at the ceiling.

Hundreds of herbs, meat and other supplies were hanging. A warm fire crackled in the hearth. Thousands of bottles lined the walls, and a small bed, along with a few bookshelves were tucked into the corner.

Natone hurried into the second room in the hut. Mike couldn't see inside the second room very well. All he could see was a pile of endless clutter. Mike was surprised to see a winding staircase up to a loft above.

Mike sat down on a decaying bench; his friends did the same (all except Hamlin who hurried into the second room to help her mother.) A table was pushed to the side of the room. Mike looked down at the floor. Pine needles and dirt hid the stones underneath.

Natone and Hamlin came back carrying… Mike wasn't sure what they were. A type of drink he supposed. Mike was handed his drink. He took a big sip and immediately gagged.

A cold draft hit Mike's face.

"Curse those damm windows!" cursed Natone. She hurried to close a few cracked windows. For a few minutes, all the noise came from the crackling of the hearth and the whistling of the wind.

Natone finally re-entered the room and sat down. "So, Daughter, what brings you back?" Natone asked, addressing Hamlin.

Hamlin's face grew serious. " Mother, we need to find the heirloom of Devil, the gem."

"Devil! What would you want with him?" exclaimed Natone.

"I will tell you later. Just tell me, Mother. I know you know where it is," inquired Hamlin.

Natone barked a laugh. "The Gem is not an heirloom! It is a portal! A portal to Earth!"

Chapter Thirteen
The Fall

Mike's stomach dropped for two reasons: one, Natone knew about Earth, and, two, Lord Devil had access to a portal.

Liva frowned. "How do you know about Earth?" she questioned.

Natone smiled. (Was Mike imagining it or did Natone hesitate before answering?)

"Sweetie, I make it my personal business to know all the secrets of the universe. I am, of course, the Hag of Leaves," Natone said with pride.

"Mother!" complained Hamlin. She shot her mother with an ice stare.

"Of course, back to the point! As you know, the Temple of the Gem is in No Man's Land," explained Natone. "All you need to do is get the gem before Devil gets it. The Gem will present an excellent way to get you back to earth before it is destroyed--before your parents worry too much!" finished Natone.

Hamlin frowned. "Mother, I do not recall you saying anything about Earth."

Natone silenced her daughter with a glare. "I will send you on your way with the supplies you need."

***

Two hours later, Hamlin and Natone had finished saying good-bye, and Thrisa was loaded up with the packages Natone had given them. Just as Mike was boarding Thrisa and Liva was clambering onto Hamlin's raft, Natone called out to her daughter: "Hamlin, wait!" Hamlin hesitated, then left Liva, and went to her mother's side.

"Hamlin," whispered Natone. "After this, you do not need to go back to war. Come home." Natone's voice was strained.

"Mother, I am out there," Hamlin's voice was stern but gentle as she pried her hands loose from her mother's steel grip.

As they took to the sky, Mike looked back one last time at the barren landscape. Natone stood outside her hut waving goodbye. Just before they went out of sound range, Mike heard Natone shout two last words: "Beware the Pup!"

***

As Thrisa was soaring over Triangle Woods, Mike called over the whipping winds, "You know, we have an island called No Mans Land back in my world."

"Really?" called Thrisa. "Weird!"

"Duck!" shrieked Hamlin suddenly. Mike barely had time to duck down low on Thrisa's golden fur before countless arrows swished past his ear.

"NOOOOO!"

Thrisa was impaled by an arrow. It hit her wing and caused her to plummet to the ground. All Mike could do was hold on for dear life. Thrisa continued to plummet to the ground.

Mike hit the ground; Thrisa fell next to him. Mike looked up dazed. All his bones hurt. He tried to move but he yelped in pain. His spine was broken. Mike's vision swam, black spots danced before his eyes.

Thrisa moaned weakly beside him.

Hamlin and Liva rushed over. Hamlin crouched beside him, her auburn hair fell into his face. He blacked out.

Mike awakened to the smell of something burning. Mike's eyes flickered open. He was lying on a bed of leaves inside a tent. To his amazement, he realized he was surrounded by flames. His amazement was quickly replaced by fear when he realized his bed was patrolled by wolves. Mike tried to scream but his throat was dry. He tried to move, but he couldn't.

A middle-aged woman hurried into the tent. She was tall, her ears were strange and pointed, her dress was made entirely out of leaves, her hair was done up in a tight bun, and she had green eyes.

When Mike was finally able to relax, he took in their surroundings. They were in a makeshift tent. Soft heather littered the floor, and he could hear laughter coming from outside.

"What thou have here?" asked a cold voice.

The tall lady scampered up against the tent wall. She bowed low to the tent entrance. A dark figure entered the tent. He had strange pointed ears, cold eyes and a billowing cloak. An amulet swung from his neck. The wolves didn't bother the newcomer. Instead, they pressed their pelts against him.

"Marrisa levee though," ordered the strange person (or something else.) The figure shared the same pointed ears and green eyes as the tall lady who had just left the tent. The figure in the cloak loomed over Mike as he struggled to rise. All the blood rushed to Mike's head as he sat up. The figure's pale face swam in and out of his vision. The figure stepped into the fire. The flames licked his legs, but he gave no notice that he was on fire.

"Thou man awake," hissed the figure.

"Wha-who are you?" choked Mike. He caught himself before he said, "What are you?"

"What thou?" the figure hissed back. "*Ton fi son el Zareen rhdu bion see*. I am Zareen, leader of the Elves, founder of the Tonans Camp, and thee Mike Lukowski. I heard much about thou."

Chapter Fourteen
Tonan's Camp

"He's an Elf. I am in an Elf's Camp! My friends! I hope they are ok." These thoughts circled through Mike's head as he stared at the stony face of the Elf leader.

"How-how do you know my name?" managed Mike.

"Thee told me," answered Zareen. As he gestured towards the flap, Hamlin and Liva burst in.

"Liva!" he cried happily as he bounded from his bed and embraced his friend.

Liva smiled happily at him. "I thought you were dead!" A dark shadow crossed Liva's face as she recalled Kirk's death. Sadness twisted in Mike's stomach. He noticed that Liva's eyes had dark bags under them and tear marks were visible on her face.

"What... where's Thrisa?" asked Mike looking around the tent, expecting to see Thrisa's head pop through the flap at any second. But to his horror, Hamlin lowered her head in grief.

"No, no! Not Thrisa, no…" Mike cried. He leaned his shoulder into Hamlin's, not caring how Liva looked at him expectantly. Everyone he knew and got close to were disappearing like smoke.

Zareen re-entered the tent. Mike carefully dried his tears. He would have time to mourn later. Zareen gave Mike a funny look but didn't press it.

"Marleen show thou camp," Zareen ordered. "Marleen! Son wk el ven fdses," shouthed Zareen in his native language.

A stunningly pretty elf sauntered into the tent. She shared the same features as Zareen. She wore a dress of leaves and her hazelnut hair fell down in a long braid. She had olive skin and piercing eyes.

"Son fln don thans fhs hla?" Marleen asked the elf king.

"Son Mike yen Hamlin yen Liva, alsn hums Hamlin sorcer," answered Zareen.

"Does she speak English? Wonder if they are related," wondered Mike.

"Hums! yen sorcer!" Marleen nearly shouted.

"Calm, Daughter," soothed Zareen. "No sen sf."

"Scont tu re? Sedg fjs om fsfvd1," demanded Marleen. "I will do so if thou want," said Marleen as she glared at her father.

"Zen!" exclaimed Zareen. "Show camp zen tents," he ordered.

"Yes… Baba," hissed Marleen.

She motioned for Mike and the others to follow her out of the tent. They left the tent with Marleen throwing a look of deep loathing at Zareen as they left.

Mike was dazzled as they stepped out of the tent. They were in a huge clearing with hundreds of tents in a circle surrounding a massive bonfire (even though it was broad daylight.) The tent they had just left had a large wooden sign on the front of it that read: Kaka Son hun.

"What does that sign say?" asked Mike to Mareen. Marleen looked startled, but she answered nonetheless. "Healers hut," Marleen said in a voice barely over a whisper. Mike expected her tone to be hard, but to his immense surprise, her voice was light and soft.

"Mike, is it not?" Marleen asked in the same soft voice.

"Yes," Mike replied plainly. He felt overshadowed by Marleen's soft, yet firm, tone and opposing stare. As they neared the edge of the camp, Marleen issued a warning: "Never go beyond camp. Triangle Woods is not a safe place. Go in you do, do not come out."

Mike shuddered as he peered through the deep woods. He remembered not too long ago when Cand and himself ran through Spook Woods to escape Hown and his gang. He realized that it was foolish, and even stupid, when they met Flint. They hardly considered what was going on. They burst in.

As Mike stared into the dense forest around him, a strange voice seemed to tell him to find Cand and destroy Lord Devil. Lost in his own thoughts, Mike didn't notice Mareen creep up behind him and place a cold pale hand on his shoulder.

"Time go," she whispered in his ear. He allowed her to lead him back to Hamlin and Liva. For a second, Mike looked around in bewilderment, wondering where Thrisa was. The truth came crashing down upon him all at once. Thrisa was dead; he would never talk to her again.

"Are you ok?" asked Liva.

Mike nodded and answered, "Sure, I'm ok, just tired." Mike said it, but he knew he was nowhere near being ok. He was worried for his brother and Mike cursed himself for going into the Stanchess.

"What prayer is 'I'm?'" inquired Marleen.

"You should rest," suggested Liva, ignoring Marleen.

"Yes," Marleen hissed. With one sweeping movement, she turned on her heel and walked away, signaling for them to follow. As they hurried after Marleen, Mike fell into pace with Hamlin.

"Where's Thrisa's b-b-ody?" shuddered Mike. It was hard to think of the little gorgelina as dead.

Hamlin gestured at a small tent not too far away. "Mike, there is something you should know," pressed Hamlin.

"Not now, I need to rest. Tell me in the morning," answered Mike. He hurried after Liva and Marleen. The last thing he saw before going into the tent was Hamlin's wounded face.

Mike disappeared inside the tent that Marleen and Liva had gone into. Mike hit himself to make sure he wasn't dreaming. The inside of the tent was magnificent! On the outside, it was barely big enough for three people. Inside, it resembled a tavern, much like the one he went into in Blan Tavern.

"I went into the inn in Blan Tavern with Liva, Kirk and Thrisa and now there is only Liva left! What did I drag them into?" Mike thought bitterly.

Mike raised his head and looked around. He was in a wide room with many tables spread around. In the very middle was a bar with a tall elf wearing a velvet cloak, polishing glasses. On the ceiling and walls were various trophies and animal heads. A few burly elves were sitting around the bar laughing and drinking.

Mike looked down expecting to see the tarp of a tent floor, but instead he glimpsed hard stone underneath a coating of moss. Mike spotted Marleen and Liva waiting impatiently at the end of the room where a spiral staircase awaited them. He moved to catch up with them, and suddenly the tall elf from the bar slammed down the glass he was polishing and blocked Mike's way.

"Zerrr is a human I thou pub, what zat?" the tall elf questioned.

"Just passing through," mumbled Mike. Marleen shouldered her way through the gathering crowd of elves.

"Ohearen! This not thou fight! " Marleen cried. "Ev Ohearen on tgh," Marleen repeated in the elven language.

Ohearen ignored Marleen. Mike glanced uneasily from side to side. Crowds of elves were crowding around Ohearen, Mike and Marleen. Mike could see Liva trying to get to the front of the crowd. Before Mike could call a warning to stay back, a shout interrupted him. He looked around wildly.

The crowd of burly elves had shoved their way to the front of the crowd and now stood behind Ohearen. Mike finally got a good look at them. They towered seven feet tall and they reminded him of the Wrestlers. They had only a loincloth on and sweat dripped from their bare shoulders. They had beady eyes and beefy hands. The look in their eyes told Mike one thing: they would kill if they needed to.

Ohearen smiled and shoved Marleen aside. As he did so, the crowd began to chant, "Ha noi! Ha noi! Ha noi!"

Mike searched for the burst of strength he got from the Wrestlers and the bounty hunters, but he felt nothing. Ohearen kicked Mike down and then reached down and grabbed him by his shirt collar.

"Do la na te!" cried a desperate voice.

Ohearen dropped Mike. He skidded on the floor until he came to rest by the backs of burly elves. They growled and grumbled but paid him no attention. Mike's vision swam but he struggled to his feet. Liva had made her way to the front of the crowd and was desperately trying to do a spell. "Do la na te!" she tried over and over again, but nothing happened. Mike tried to fight back, but he couldn't find the strength.

Mike felt a sharp pain in his back. He staggered forward into the waiting arms of Ohearen. He tackled Mike, pinning his arms behind his back. Ohearen held him tightly, forcing him to his knees. Mike looked up at the grinning face of a short elf with yellow teeth and pasty skin. He was wielding a club.

Ohearen shoved him into the middle of the floor and a mouthful of blood formed in Mike's mouth. He heard Liva shout, "No!" and

Marleen desperately struggled against the elves holding her.

The short elf raised his club. Mike closed his eyes preparing for the final blow.

"Stop!" shrieked a voice.

Chapter Fifteen
The Storm

It was Hamlin. She strode into the room. A green cloak was strung over her shoulders and pinned with a silver clasp.

"Stop!" she repeated.

"Why thee listen to thou?" asked Ohearen. He had abandoned Mike's limp form and was creeping towards Hamlin.

"Because you have no choice," Hamlin calmly countered. She allowed violet flames to grow in her hands. The elves cowered away from it.

Mike's head hit the floor. Through his eyelids, he saw blast after blast of violet light. He fainted.

When Mike came to his senses, he was laying on a huge cream colored horse that was galloping into the Triangle Woods. Mike lifted his head slightly and looked around. Thick trees surrounded him and obscured the sky. He was shocked to notice that Hamlin and Liva were also riding on the horse.

"Not again!" Mike thought savagely. They were on the run again because of him. Mike twisted his head. He was shocked to notice that Zareen and Marleen were on a slender chestnut horse not too far away.

"Mike! You're alive!" Liva cried joyfully. She twisted in her seat to hug Mike. Mike struggled into a seated position on the saddle.

"Mike, I am glad you are fine," Hamlin said coolly. Something about the coldness in Hamlin's tone frightened Mike.

"Um... where am I?" asked Mike.

"Once you blacked out, the Elves went crazy. They started attacking us. They wouldn't stop until Hamlin burned Ohearen," explained Liva. She showed Mike a long thin cut on her arm.

"Wouldn't she have healed herself by now?" Mike thought, puzzled.

"Liva, can't you heal yourself? With your magic?" Mike ventured.

Liva hung her head, her dark hair covering her face. "I'm sorry I couldn't save you. Our powers don't work..." Liva said sadly.

"What!" exploded Mike.

"They don't work- IN THE CAMP!" finished Liva.

"Oh," Mike muttered.

"And I guess SOMEONE didn't tell me," Liva looked savagely at Marleen and Zareen.

Zareen pulled the horse closer so they galloped beside the chestnut horse that Mike, Liva and Hamlin were on.

"What?" asked Marleen once she was under Liva's withering stare.

Mike noticed that Marleen had a big bruise on the side of her face and Zarleen had ripped off a part of his cloak and used it as a sling. Hamlin seemed to be the only one not harmed.

"They were harmed protecting me," Mike realized suddenly.

"Thou have force field," Zareen explained.

"Huh," Mike mumbled.

"Repels magic," Marleen answered.

That's when Mike realized that Zareen's amulet was absent from his neck.

"You--your-- nevermind," Mike tried to tell Zarleen about his amulet but thought better of it.

That's when the first clap of thunder shook the trees around them. Mike gripped the coarse hairs of the horse. It neighed in protest but Mike held on. The wind began to pick up and water droplets the size of marbles dropped from the sky as thunder rumbled above.

"Can this world even get thunderstorms?" Mike cried over the whipping wind.

"No!" Replied Hamlin, "That's absurd! We get--" Suddenly a dark black shape fell from the sky, shaking tree branches, and causing them to shiver as they landed. The whole ground seemed to shake. The commotion and shaking of the ground caused the horses to stumble, but they went on galloping.

"Storm thons," finished Hamlin.

"What the heck is that?" shrieked Liva.

Another dark shape fell from the sky directly in front of them. The shape made a huge crater in the ground.

The horses skidded to a stop. Twenty or so shapes crawled out of the crater. Hamlin lit a small flame in the palm of her hand, illuminating the creatures. They had jet black fur and sharp fangs dripping with drool. They had purple shoulder spikes that dripped with venom. The horses tossed their manes in fear and pawed the ground.

"Strom thons," breathed Marleen.

"Retreat!" cried Zareen.

He pulled the reins of the slender horse. Mike, Liva, Hamlin, Marleen and Zareen turned, preparing to flee. Thirty more shapes crawled out of the darkness surrounding the horses.

Chapter Sixteen
Survive

Mike's breath caught in his throat as he stared at the storm thons.

"We come peace," Zareen tried.

A storm thon, slightly bigger than the rest, paced forward so it was directly in front of the horses. It had a ring of thorns around its neck, unusual gray fur, shoulder spikes dripping with venom, neck fur bristling and its lips were pulled back in a snarl. It was ready to attack.

"Who…" it snarled.

"Wha…" Mike thought bewildered.

Zarleen dipped his head in acknowledgment: "Queen Arenes."

"Thou mean no harm," Marleen attempted to sooth the bristling Queen.

A second storm thon stepped up beside Queen Arenes. He was smaller than the queen but bigger than the average storm thon. He shared the same gray fur as Queen Arenes. He had an anklet of thorns and dark circles around his eyes and long thin scars wound their way down his back.

"Move… on…," the scared storm thon growled in Queen Arenes' ear.

"No! Rumberet!" Queen Arenes shot back.

Rumberet dipped his head in obedience and backed up into the wall of snarling storm thons.

"We just want to pass! Jeez!," Liva grumbled with an eye roll. It was the wrong thing to say.

"Storms thons!... Attack!" ordered Queen Arenes.

A swarm of black fur hit Mike. All he could see and smell was fur and sweat. But for some reason the storm thons couldn't harm him. Their teeth broke on his skin and their claws glanced harmlessly against him. The storm thons backed cautiously away from Mike.

"You… have… heir…throne… of Devil," growled Queen Arenes.

All the storm thons gradually backed away from the travelers. To Mike's bewilderment, they began to bow.

"Defeat… him… win all doing… respect," Remberet concluded.

The storm thons parted in a respectful line allowing the travelers to pass.

Once the horses were a safe distance from the storm thons and their menacing leader, Mike could ponder what had happened. He stared down at his arms where the storm thons had tried to scratch and harm him; his arms didn't bear one wound.

In the distance Mike could make out the faint outline of a ginormous temple.

Suddenly, the horses skidded to a stop. They were in a deserted clearing with a single tree, soft grass and a small river gently gurgling its way through the woods. The horses neighed and pawed the ground.

"What's happening? Why have we stopped?" grumbled Liva.

Mike looked at Liva for the first time since escaping the storm thons: Liva's shoulder length hair was dotted with leaves and twigs, her face was smeared with dirt and she had several scratches running up the length of her arms.

"Thou reached border," explained Zareen.

Marleen gracefully slipped off her horse's back. The others did the same until Mike was the only one left. He tried to do the same graceful move as Marleen but ended up tangling himself in the bridle. Once he had gotten free, Mike staggered over to Liva.

"What now?" asked Mike, eager to move.

"Rest," replied Zareen.

Mike grinded his teeth in frustration. He didn't want to wait for Lord Devil to destroy the world, but he kept his mouth shut. He trailed silently behind Liva and Zareen when they went to unpack the dwindling supplies.

Tents were thrown on the ground bursting into full fledged houses.

"Female zat one male tat one," commanded Zareen pointing to two identical tents. Hamlin shrugged and ducked into one of the tents without a word to the others. Zareen hesitated but pushed aside the flap for the opposite tent and swept in.

Liva bid Mike good night and followed Hamlin into the tent. The clearing was then empty except for Marleen and Mike.

"Walk with me," offered Marleen beckoning for Mike.

Mike gazed out at the unfamiliar trees looming above--it wasn't his idea of fun.

"Ok…" he answered slowly.

"I protect," Marleen murmured soothingly.

Not sure what she meant, Mike followed her into the darkening forest. Gnarled roots blocked their path and insects bit and scratched their skin.

Suddenly, Marleen came to an abrupt stop. Startled, Mike stopped behind her. Marleen turned to face him, her hair blowing in the slight breeze of wisdom, and experience shown in her eyes. It was in that spot that Mike realized how extraordinarily beautiful she truly was.

"Mike…" Marleen started her voice calm and soothing. Marleen gently touched her hand to Mike's cheek. He felt his face burn at her touch, but for once, he didn't care. Her hand was cool and light like a feather.

"Mike tho hero," Marleen murmured softly.

"I don't know…" he mumbled. He felt awkward and big next to Marleen's gentle form.

"I'll go to the end of the world for you, Mike," Marleen confessed with no trace of an accent.

"You-you speak English?" spluttered Mike. Marleen laughed a soft feathery laugh.

"Yes." Then she leaned forward and kissed him. He didn't know if the kiss lasted a second or an hour. When they finally broke apart, her face was flushed and her eyes glowed with happiness.

"Oh, am I interrupting something?" asked a curt voice. Mike whirled around. Standing behind him was Hamlin, her eyes aglow with anger.

Chapter Seventeen
Recollections

"What are you doing?" spat Hamlin.

"Collecting firewood," Marleen answered simply, without a trace of regret in her voice.

"You know perfectly well that I can light a fire with a flick of my wrist," spat Hamlin.

Marleen was suddenly on her feet, her eyes blazing with anger. "Not all species can do that, Sorcerer!" snarled Marleen.

"Oh, forgive me Elf!" Hamlin shot back. "Should have known."

Mike backed away carefully. The women took notice of him. Then he turned tail and sprinted into the forest once he knew he was out of earshot of the screeching women. He leaned on a tree panting. "I shouldn't have done that," Mike thought nervously. Not looking back, Mike headed back to the campsite.

***

The women had not returned when Mike staggered back into the campsite. Mike cast himself down on the soft grass next to the girl tent.

Suddenly a loud sniff came from inside the girls tent. Wondering what on earth it could be, Mike hauled himself to his feet and ducked under the swinging flap of the tent. Mike recoiled in shock when he took in the surroundings of the tent. He gaped at the supposedly small tent.

Instead of being cramped and small, it was the size of a large apartment. It had crimson walls dotted with odd paintings and designs, bunks spiraled to the ceiling, and torches lined the walls causing the tent to fall into a sort of eerie glow.

A loud sniff brought Mike back to earth, ripping his gaze from the artwork dotted along the tent walls. He searched for the sound and soon located it. A large lump was curled up in a deserted bunk. Mike stepped forward tentatively.

"Liva?" he asked into the darkness, his voice barely higher than a whisper. Rising her head from a mountain of blankets and pillows, Liva fixed him with an unblinking stare. Her

144

normally vibrant face was splotchy with tears and her hair fell in bunches.

"Mike?" Liva asked, her voice radiated with unsureness.

"What's wrong?" inquired Mike.

Liva staired miserably down at the tent floor.

"Kirk," muttered Liva unexpectedly. Mike's stomach twisted in an odd sort of way.

"What?" he asked, knowing perfectly what she was going to say.

"KIRK!" Liva spat anger now. It vibrated off her in waves. "Why did he have to die!" her voice rose to a wail. "Why…" her voice was now softer than a whisper.

"You loved him, didn't you?" Mike said softly.

Not looking up, Liva nodded into her hands. "Yes," she whispered, still not looking up. "I've loved him since we were nine. He never seemed to like me the same," Liva confessed. Her tone was still miserable.

Mike froze; he never realized his friend had been in love for so long.

"I never thought I would see Cand again... I might still not," Mike whispered, his eyes on the floor.

Liva looked up, startled at his sudden recollection.

"There was a time when he made me swim in the lake in the middle of January," Mike recalled. Liva made a noise halfway between a sob and a laugh.

Mike remembered a moment many years before. "Remember that time that we went fishing by ourselves for the first time? Kirk was so mad he pushed me off the boat. And then--"

"Cand fished you out with a pole," finished Liva.

"I miss him," muttered Liva.

"Me too."

"MIKE! LIVA!" cried a voice, desperation etched in every syllable.

Mike swiveled his head so fast he heard a crack. Standing in the entrance to the tent was

Zareen, breathless. "It-it Marleen she disappeared!" Zareen gasped.

Chapter Eighteen
Disappearances

"What?!?" spat Mike.

"Marleen!" replied Zareen frustrated.

Liva slipped gracefully off the bunk. "When did you last see her?" she asked in a hollow whisper. Though concern sparked in her eyes.

"Near Triangle Woods," murmured Zareen.

Liva bounded off to look in the woods. Mike moved to follow her, but Zareen thrust a hand out preventing Mike from going any farther.

"Mike, she took my amulet with her." Zareen said smoothly. There was no trace of an accent.

"You too?" moaned Mike.

Zareen smiled faintly. "All elves speak fluent English. We speak it; it is in our genes."

"Why?" asked Mike, perplexed.

"To hide ourselves from other races. If the elves pretend to be dimwitted, then we won't be targeted. The elves only reveal themselves when they are certain they can trust you," Zareen explained. Zareen looked down his long pointed nose at Mike. "Marleen revealed herself then?" It was more of an accusation than a question.

Zareen swore suddenly, *"Curse her!"*

"What?" Mike said loudly. Zareen was now frowning deeply.

"Mike, can you understand me?" Zareen asked, his voice deeply troubled.

"Of course!" Mike scoffed. *"You're speaking English now, aren't you?"* Mike growled. He was deeply offended that Zareen and the rest of the elves had not told him that they spoke fluent English.

"No, I'm not," Zareen whispered quietly.

"What?!? Of course you are!" Some of the fear that Mike felt leaked into his words.

"No, I am speaking Elvish," Zareen announced. "There is only one possibility…" murmured Zareen more to himself than Mike.

"How can I speak Elvish?" Mike wondered to himself.

"Mike, there is only one possibility," Zareen repeated.

"Oh great, now I'm some mythical elf. You know I should be used to it by now," scoffed Mike.

"No, Mike, you must be an elf," Zareen declared.

All the heat in the world seemed to crash into him and the ground swam lazily beneath his feet. *"An elf... no, it's impossible,"* Mike thought distractedly.

"You have to be, Mike. There is no other explanation." Zareen said confidently.

"Worry about *that* later," decided Mike, but he knew he wouldn't be able to put his brain at a pause. Shoving Zareen's theories to the back of his mind, he addressed the more complicated problem.

"So… Marleen took your amulet…." Mike began slowly not believing it.

"Yes!" snarled Zareen. "I gave it to her!"

Mike waved his arms distractedly. "Why did you give it to her then?" he asked with a raised eyebrow.

"I had my reasons," Zareen murmured hastily.

"What does the amulct do?" asked Mike, momentarily distracted by curiosity.

"It enables the wearer to shapeshift," Zareen said distractedly.

"Heck, that's a bad thing to lose," muttered Mike.

"Guys, you should see this," called a voice from outside the tent.

Liva was standing, open mouth staring at the sky. Hamlin was beside her. Identical versions of amazement were plastered on their faces.

Mike followed their gaze: a good twenty feet away was the most abstract building Mike had ever seen. It was the size of a large tree house. It had colorful streamers bursting from the sides, and it was painted with millions of different colors. Steep steps led up to a small balcony that led into the building. An open ledge with a fire pit protruded from the side of it.

A slight brush on the side of his shoulder showed the entrance of Zareen. His face was flustered with worry for his daughter and his amulet. Zareen's gaze became unfocused and then disbelieving. He stared at the building with disbelief etched in every line of his face.

"Impossible! We were miles from it a second ago....." declared Liva. She trailed off. "We were miles from it....." she repeated wonderingly.

"It must have moved somehow," decided Mike, more to himself than the others.

"No," Zareen said firmly. His voice returned to his crisp accent.

As they all stared at the wanderers building in front of them, Hamlin marched to stand in front of the group.

"Do you want to say it or should I?" Hamlin snapped when the others looked at each other in confusion. She just rolled her eyes in exasperation.

"Welcome to the Temple of the Gem."

Chapter Nineteen
The Temple of the Gem

"B-but the temple…" Mike trailed off.

"Well, we are here now. I say we go and get you home," Hamlin announced, avoiding Mike's eye.

"What?!? I thought we would help you with the Soul Flames! And CAND! What about him?" Mike nearly shouted.

"Thou find Cand. Send thee home after," Zareen explained, his voice once more carpeted by accent.

"The Soul Flames are OUR problem, not yours," Hamlin said in a final voice.

Mike didn't argue any further.

***

Twenty minutes later, with the tents packed up, the group entered the Temple of the Gem in a stony silence. They walked through the hallways with no trouble at all. Marble caged them in on all sides and staircases twisted to the unknown.

Finally, they reached the balcony. It had a large pit with flames flickering weakly on a dais.

There stood a large statue of a gargoyle. It had long curved claws and an evil smile. Embedded in its chest, was a scarlet gem glowing brightly.

The balcony was big enough for six people. Seven feet below was the pebbly ground that stretched for miles. A large ring encircled the temple. In the distance, he could make out Lord Devil's castle.

"Cand," murmured his mind.

A cold hand suddenly clasped his shoulder. Startled, he turned. Hamlin stood behind him. "Come," she whispered, her voice glancing off the marble. Mike allowed her to lead him away. They stopped when Mike was certain they were alone. "Mike, there is something I need to tell you before you go-" a loud scream cut off Hamlin's last retort.

"Liva," muttered Mike as he set off on a run with Hamlin close on his heels.

They arrived back at the balcony, panting. Liva crouched over the statue, "Mike! Look at this!" Liva called.

With a last glance at the disgruntled Hamlin, Mike joined Liva at the foot of the statue. "What is it, Liva?" he asked in a tired voice.

"Look! It's a dog!" squealed Liva.

Sure enough, a small golden puppy crouched at the foot of the statue. It had large green eyes and fixated on them with an unblinking stare. As Liva reached to pet it, a sense of foreboding surged through Mike's veins. A warning floated to the top of his head: *"Beware the pup!"*

"Liva! NO!" he cried, but it was too late. Liva reached to pet the dog. The second her hand came in contact with the dog's curly hair, a low rumbling sound filled the temple.

"That did *not* sound good," Hamlin whispered. Liva and Mike slowly backed away from the statue and joined Zareen and Hamlin.

The rumbling sounded again, closer than before. Suddenly, thick iron chains burst from the gargoyle, wrapping themselves around Liva and Zareen and pulling them to the ground.

"LIVA!" cried Mike at the same time Hamlin shouted, "ZAREEN!"

They rushed to help their friends, turning their backs on the doorway. Suddenly the ground erupted. Mike fell into Hamlin's arms and tried to shield himself, Zareen and Liva, who were too tightly bound to do anything. Rubble showered down upon them.

Still with Hamlin by his side, Mike pushed off the majority of the rubble and helped Hamlin to her feet. Her beautiful eyes connected with his and she gave the smallest of nods.

Mike's mind cleared. Without thinking, he hugged Hamlin. Hamlin looked startled but didn't protest.

"I might barf," said a drawling voice.

Mike and Hamlin whirled around. Standing in the doorway was Lord Devil. Instead of a six piece suit, he wore a billowing jet black cloak with gold trimming.

Then Mike saw something, but he must have been imagining it. Becuse there was know way it was possible.

159

Because standing next to Lord Devil was someone Mike never expected to see again.

"No, impossible," murmured Hamlin.

Chapter Twenty
The Many Betrayals

It was Natone, the Hag of Leaves, who stood beside Lord Devil. She wore a long dress made entirely of plants and her hair was tied in a tight bun.

"Mother. What are you doing with *him*?" asked Hamlin, shrilly pointing at Lord Devil.

Natone grinned broadly. "Hamlin, have you ever wondered who your father was?" asked Natone in a high clear voice.

"What? Wha- no, NO!" Realization hit Hamlin like a brick load of stone.

Mike suddenly realized *Lord Devil* was Hamlin's father. Without thinking, Mike reached out and grasped Hamlin's hand.

"Daughter, come join us," offered Lord Devil.

Hamlin looked down at her hand with Mike's and then at her parents' faces. She looked at Natone. "You raised me," she murmured, looking at her feet.

"Yes," said Natone almost as softly as her daughter.

Hamlin looked up, her eyes alight.

"Come daughter. Come to the right side." goaded Lord Devil.

"No."

"What!" spat Natone.

Hamlin's face was calm ferocity. "No."

"You're making a mistake, Daughter," cautioned Lord Devil.

"I am no daughter of yours."

"Fine," Natone spoke with menace in her voice.

Natone clapped her hands together once and twice. Liva and Zareen rose into the air suspended by invisible ropes.

"Hamlin…" Mike spoke warningly. Hamlin nodded as she understood the caution in his voice. They edged under Zareen and Liva as if to catch them if they fell. Fear twisted in his belly. He couldn't let another close friend fall.

Lord Devil motioned behind him. Emerging from the darkness were all Mike's nightmares combined. Hordes of Dominions of Death crept out of the darkness, odd creatures

163

that looked like ogres, millions of vipers the size of pineapples, cloaked figures crawled out, and other horrors he couldn't describe. Lord Devil's army assembled behind him. Leering faces snarled at him from every direction. He edged closer to Hamlin.

Suddenly, two Dominions of Death approached Lord Devil. In between them was a ragged form that Mike hardly recognized.

"CAND!" he gasped. Cand looked so different than when he had last seen him. Cand's clothes were ragged and his cheeks hollow. Deep gashes ran their way up his back and face.

"MIKE!" cried Cand. Relief flooded his face.

"Devil's castle is so cool! Hey, didja know that he's a gr--" Cand began excitedly.

"Enough," said Lord Devil, firmly cutting off Cand.

Lord Devil pointed his finger at Cand. A large gash appeared on the side of Cand's face. He gave a cry of pain and crumpled to the ground. The Dominions of Death left him in a heap and returned to their ranks.

Natone appeared leering at Cand. She suspended him in the air so he hovered above them next to Liva and Zareen.

Suddenly Lord Devil's army parted to let a straggle of people supported by Dominions of Death walk by. Three ragged people were thrown at Lord Devil's feet.

"I still don't see why you are doing this," said Thoran plainly.

"I do. He's an idiot, that's why," decided Tothan.

The third figure just moaned weakly.

Devil's army muttered nervously but didn't break ranks.

"Natone levitated them into the air like she had done for Cand, Liva and Zareen.

Suddenly the third figure turned over. To Mike's complete surprise, he recognized him: "HOWN!"

"That idiot who--" Liva was cut off and Natone had levitated her toward the statue.

There was a sickening crack, and Liva crumbled to the ground.

"LIVA!" Fear for his friend blinded him. He charged forward only to be repelled back into Hamlin's arms.

Natone pointed her hand at Cand. He awoke and began screaming. Cand's cries tore at Mike's heart. "Stop!" he cried.

The levitated bodies fell in a heap beside Liva.

The Dominions of Death reached hungrily for Hamlin and Mike. Terrified, Mike clutched Hamlin's hand. Her eyes glowed red and she rose into the air bringing Mike along with her.

"Start it," ordered Lord Devil.

Natone at his side, they dragged the prisoners into the middle and his army made a ragged circle around him.

"You called," said a clear voice from behind the army.

"Yes, come hear, Marleen," hissed Lord Devil.

Chapter Twenty-One
Sacrifice

Marleen sauntered onto the balcony, Zareen's amulet swinging from her nest.

"Do the magic," ordered Lord Devil.

Marleen's betrayal crashed into Mike like a stone. "No… NO!" he cried, burying his head in Hamlin's shoulder.

"Mike, listen to me. I am going to attack them," Hamlin said quietly. All Mike could do was nod.

Marleen opened her hands and spoke: *"On ladvd fdh af ds…"* The gem in the statue rumbled and broke free. A fine trickle of dust issued from it. The gem landed in the middle and hovered there.

And from his hands, Lord Devil produced the Soul Flames. Throwing them down, they engulfed the gem. The hostages' eyes were wide with fear as the flames grew higher.

"Hamlin," Mike murmured softly, for Natone had begun pulling them in. A faint door had begun to appear, becoming stronger by the second.

Cand began to scream. An image suddenly flickered into existence. It was Earth but something was wrong. It was smoking, burning.

The door suddenly swung open and a tall man walked out. He had scraggly black hair, an upturned nose and wore a thin jacket made of leather.

"Father," breathed Lord Devil.

"Danial, I never wanted this. Never wanted this," Lord Devil's father began to fade.

"No, NO!" shrieked Lord Devil. He attempted to grab his father but it was no use. He gave a shriek and plunged head first into the door.

Then silence. Mike thought of Kirk and how much he missed him. Suddenly, another figure burst out the door.

"Kirk?" breathed Liva with uncertainty.

The figure came into the light. It was indeed Kirk. Liva flung herself into Kirk's pale arms and they kissed. When they broke apart, Liva flushed scarlet but smiled. Kirk hugged her one last time and began to fade. He looked at Mike.

"Thank you for bringing me back," Kirk said in a hollow voice. Mike barely had time to process Kirk's last words, for Natone had snuck up on him, thrown Mike to the ground with a strong arm and wrapped her arms around his throat.

"H-Hamlin!" he choked.

She was there, throwing Natone off with one swipe of her arm. She faced her mother; anger shone in her eyes. Suddenly, the moon slid out from under a cloud. Fire burned in Hamlin's eyes. Hamlin levitated into the air with one swift move. She knocked Natone away, throwing her off the balcony.

Hamlin landed on the ground windswept and stumbled into his arms, not caring that they were in battle or that they had been so cold earlier. Mike kissed her there, lips met and they only broke apart when sharp fangs connected with his back.

Marleen had transformed into a shaggy great wolf. She sank her fangs into his back. With a roar of pain, he tried to shake her off, but it was no use. Suddenly, newfound strength coursed through him. Throwing Marleen from his back, he sprang up. He pinned her to the ground and she transformed into her real self. Wrenching Zareen's amulet from her neck, he loosened his grip, allowing her to scamper away into the night. Mike scrambled back to his friends as Devil's army closed in.

"You need to get to the portal! NOW!" cried Hamlin as she blasted one of the Dominions of Death away.

"NO! I am not leaving you."

"Me neither," declared Liva.

"I'm not leaving you," repeated Mike. Liva nodded slowly.

Suddenly, a great blast erupted from the ground, shoving them backwards. Rubble rained down on him. He groped to find Liva and pull her to safety. Lord Devil's army was bearing down on them with their master gone. They were untamed and ready to lash out on anyone. Vengeance shone in their eyes, eager to avenge their fallen master. They seemed like a whole different monster with the light of battle in their eyes.

The army closed in on the Dominions of Death , bearing down, preparing to rip apart their enemies. Mike backed away to the statue. The others followed suit as they were surrounded. Mike searched for his brother, for some sort of solitude. He was there with Liva and Hamlin at his side, joined by Thoran and Tothan followed by a more reluctant Hown. At least he was with his friends when he went down. Mike grasped Hamlin's hand searching for something solid.

Suddenly, an ear-splitting shriek pierced the night. Lord Devil's army paused from bearing down on their prey. Hundreds of sleek black bodies thundered onto the balcony, climbing the steep temple walls with ease.

A particularly large creature was leading the storm of creatures. If they were to help him and his friends, or if they were reinforcements from the outskirts, Mike didn't know.

Lord Devil's army looked at the creatures with no recollection; they were no friends of Lord Devil. The army had a savage light in their eyes, momentarily forgetting about their old prey. The creatures were thrown into the light of the gem. The leader wore a circlet of thorns. The creature pounding beside her had an anklet of thorns. The storm thons had come to help. Queen Arenes and Remberet threw themselves at Lord Devil's army, giving the smallest of nods at Mike and the others.

They clashed teeth with claws, bodies with swords, ripping at flesh and scouring fur. The sky was filled with the growls and grunts of Lord Devil's army and the storm thons.

"We need to help them!" cried Mike. Though vicious and determined, the storm thons were badly outnumbered.

Hamlin shrugged. "I am not your mother." With a glance back, she threw herself into battle, knocking vipers away, burning others to a crisp.

"Cand, stay here," ordered Mike firmly. His fighting blood he had acquired was burning although he had no sword. He knew he didn't need one. With Liva by his side, he ran towards the heaving mass of bodies.

"Fine, I'll just stay here and sulk!" called Cand. A brief smile flitted across Mike's lips as he plunged into battle.

Liva shot spell after spell, using all the talent she had to keep the enemy from overwhelming her. Mike rammed into large creatures that looked like trolls, knocking them aside.

Suddenly, large hands grabbed him and shoved him to the ground, his head bouncing off the floor. Lights popped in his eyes as excruciating pain filled his body. Screaming out in pain, he writhed on the ground as if white-hot knives were pressing into his skin. And it was over as quickly as it had come. He lay panting on the ground.

Mike rolled over, and he was staring into the leering face of Ohearen. Ohearen held a white hot whip gleaming with power, and he lashed it again. Mike screamed as the white hot tip lashed his body.

Ohearen leaned close to Mike: "Teach thee to stay away from me pub," he hissed menacingly.

Half-blinded by pain, Mike kicked up, putting all his remaining strength in his kick. Ohearen staggered but didn't fall. Mike sprang to his feet. Ohearen bared down on him, whip at the ready.

"NO!"

Hamlin threw herself in front of Mike. The whip deflected with a flick of her wrist. Throwing Ohearen off balance, the brief second of confusion was enough. Throwing himself on top of Ohearen, Mike held him down and squeezed his neck. He underestimated his own strength. Ohearen turned blue. Terrified, Mike released him, but it was too late. Ohearen rolled over and didn't get up.

Horrified, Mike backed away. "He would have killed you!" shrieked Hamlin as she whirled back into the battle.

The enemy was slowly retreating against the storm thons' slashing claws and Hamlin's and Liva's spells. Flames spewed from her hands and her hair flew wild. Liva murmured incantations causing creatures to stumble and keel over unconscious.

"You… fight… good," spoke a raspy voice.

Remberet stood beside him surveying the battle. His fur was ripped and torn in some places and a nasty cut was swelling below his eye. But other than that, he was unharmed.

"I fought one dude," confessed Mike.

"You…..Kick him," pressed Remberet.

"So…." responded Mike slowly, but Remberet had already thrown himself into the battle.

Suddenly a Dominions of Death leapt on him, throwing him on the ground. He struggled in vain; the Dominions of Death's steel grip was too strong.

"I will kill you just like your friend," the Dominions of Death hissed in his ear.

It was the same Dominions of Death that had killed Kirk. Anger surged in Mike's veins. With the strongest heave he could muster, Mike threw the Dominions of Death off. Flipping around, Mike shoved it to the ground until it went limp.

A sharp scream pierced the night. "Cand," muttered Mike and rushed back to the statue.

Hown lay on the ground, blood trickling down his cheek. Cand was crouched by the statue. A large hairy beast was sinking its fangs into Cand's neck. Cand seemed to have fainted. The beast turned its leering face on Mike, saliva dripping from its salivating mouth, fangs painted with blood.

"Halana haren!" cried a voice. The beast shrank until it was the size of a small apple. It gave a pitiful shriek and fled into the night.

Liva ran to Mike; they crouched by Cand's limp form. Blood squirted from a gash in his neck. Without a word, Liva traced a hand over Cand's wound and muttered the same counter curse over and over: *"Gthan afrenne. Gthan afrenne."* The wounds began to heal and the blood seemed to re-trace itself back into the wounds.

Mike crouched behind his brother's still form. He seemed to have passed out.

"Go, help Hamlin," ordered Liva. "I'll stay with him."

Mike didn't question it and left his brother in Liva's tender hands. Mike turned to leave.

"Wait!" cried Liva as she withdrew something from beneath her. It was a sword, a beautiful sword. It had a crisscross pattern of flames and the metal gleamed a deadly iron. Mike gripped the handle; it was leather.

"Its name is Lockbite," murmured Liva. "I just built it."

Mike was shocked. "You built a sword?" he asked.

Now Liva looked defensive. "Yeah! Just go, idiot." She pushed him effectively, and he plunged back into the battle.

But now it was different. Lockbite became a meter of death hurling and slashing. His heart was pumped full of adrenaline.

Dominions of Death after Dominions of Death fell at his blade, but they kept coming, threatening to overwhelm him. Then she was there. Hamlin was at his back, flames glowing from her hands and hair flickering above her head. They fought back to back and soon they had cleared a circle no one dared approach.

"COWARDS!" shrieked a voice. Marleen was back. The amulet was gone from her neck, but her eyes were still alight with anger.

"ATTACK!" She screeched as the army surged forwards and Mike met them with Hamlin at his side. He fought like never before, throwing them aside like rag dolls, weaving through the army looking for Marleen.

Then he saw her. Marleen was creeping towards Liva and Cand. Liva was trying desperately to stop her by firing spell after spell, but nothing helped.

Marleen grabbed Liva and grappled with her. "STOP! OR SHE DIES!" Marleen's voice bounded over to Mike's ears. The battle subsided. Marleen had Liva in a headlock with a knife to her throat.

Chapter Twenty-Two
No Mercy

Time ran still as Marleen brandished the knife at Liva's throat.

And there they were: Hamlin, Zareen, Tothan, Thoran, the storm thons and, surprisingly, Hown. They were all at his side, but it did nothing for Liva; she was trapped in Marleen's grasp. Suddenly, the still form of Natone stirred. She awoke and drifted towards Marleen. The army gradually fell back as their remaining leaders gathered.

"If you move, I'll kill your friend!" spat Marleen, abandoning any trace of an accent.

"DAUGHTER!" cried Zareen. He pushed forward. He had a nasty cut swelling along the side of his face and the amulet was swinging on his chest.

Marleen looked at the amulet on his chest. "You have something that's MINE!" she shrieked, throwing herself at Zareen and dropping Liva on the ground.

Mike started forward, but Hamlin beat him to it. Crouching by her side, she placed a tentative hand on her face. Nodding slightly, Hamlin turned to her mother.

Mike and Hamlin circled her while the storm thons made a bristling line to block off the army from its leader. Zareen and Marleen were locked in combat for the amulet. "It's MINE!" shrieked Marleen with delusion.

"NO!" cried Zareen as he transformed into first a bear, then a lion. They were all lethal animals, but neither could get the upper hand.

So Mike focused on Natone. She was staring at Hamlin oddly. "Lord Devil is my husband, and he will always be my husband. And you, Child, will always be his daughter," foretold Natone.

Hamlin stared at her mother with tears in her eyes. "I AM NO DAUGHTER OF YOURS OR YOUR HUSBAND! I AM HAMLIN. THE Soul Flames ARE ME!" snarled Hamlin. She flung herself at Natone, but she was ready, throwing herself sideways. Purple flames began to flicker in Natone's hands.

Natone and Hamlin clashed. Hamlin's eyes were just red flames. She danced with fire lighting her hands, tossing fireball after fireball at her mother, but nothing seemed to stop her.

"WHO GAVE YOU THIS POWER? I DID! THE Soul Flames LIVE INSIDE YOU! BUT YOUR POWER COMES FROM THE OUTSKIRTS! YOU AND MIKE ARE THE HEIR TO THE THRONE OF LORD DEVIL!" Natone cried as she launched an attack on her daughter.

Tendrils of smoke filtered from Natone's wrist, pinning Hamlin to the ground. Hamlin struggled and Mike moved to help her. Natone thrust out a hand and an invisible barrier was flung between them. Natone tightened the tendrils around Hamlin.

"I will kill you and take the throne. Your powers are nothing compared to mine. *I am the cave where secrets lurk*," hissed Natone.

"The prophecy! That's what she means!" realized Mike.

"Tell me, Daughter, who you are," growled Natone.

Suddenly the tendrils of smoke fell from Hamlin's body. She was glowing. The moonlight reflected off her hands where nothing but fire, a trace of fear, splattered across Natone's face.

"I AM HAMLIN, AND I HAVE REACHED MY PRIME!" With those last words, light burst from Hamlin's body. Her eyes glowed, and Natone tried to scurry out of the way, but an invisible force kept her there.

Hamlin rose into the air. Her body was filled with light, and she spoke two words: "Goodbye, Mother." Her hands glowed with bright light; her hair flickered. A blinding light filled the balcony and the Hag of Leaves was gone. She was nothing but a pile of plants.

Hamlin landed on the ground. The barrier was diminished, and Mike lept into Hamlin's arms. They kissed full on the lips, submerged in each other's arms.

"I love you, Mike."

"Me too." Hamlin looked away with a distant look in her eyes.

Suddenly, a sharp scream split the air. Mike whirled around. Marleen and Zareen were still fighting. It wasn't going too well for Zareen. His face was streaked with blood and Marleen was bearing down on him. She had won herself weapons: her finger tips had long claws on them and she was hacking and slashing. Zareen was desperately trying to scoot away but she held him still, sinking her long claws into Zareen. He howled and thrashed as bubbles of blood surfaced. Marleen twisted her claws into his belly and hissed in his ear, *"Give me the amulet."*

"No!" he sputtered desperately.

Then Mike did something realy stupid or really brave. He charged forward. "STOP!" he cried.

Marleen turned to him. Her blood-stained claws glinted in the moonlight. She leapt at him with her claws outstretched.

Mike parried and feigned to the left. He didn't even know where he knew swordplay from. And they fought, fought over the spasming body of Zareen. Mike pulled and heaved, but Marleen wouldn't give up. He pushed her back. "Give up!" he cried.

Marleen just snarled at him and lunged forward. Mike pinned her to the ground with the butt of his sword. She struggled underneath him. Mike looked at Marleen's struggling form. Defiance was kindling in her eyes. "I will never give up!" she spat.

Tears sprung in his eyes as he raised his sword for the fatal blow. It never landed. Marleen grabbed his wrist and flipped him over onto his back with surprising strength. Stars popped in the back of his head. Marleen ripped her claws against Mike's shoulder and he howled as his blood squirted free. Marleen began to dig her claws into his back…

Suddenly, the moonlight hit him; his body was bathed in it. Strength forged through him. He raised Lockbite. The whole world seemed to be behind him as he transformed. He was an eagle, a bear, a lion--he could change form the second the thought appeared in his head.

Mike willed the earth to rise. He didn't know how, but he could feel a connection. He could feel the tiniest worm, the largest animal moving in the dirt below him. *"Rise, rise!"* he commanded in his mind. Power and strength, like he had never felt before, surged through him. The earth was in his veins; it was his blood. The earth tore itself free from the ground, soil and rubble raining down on them. Tendrils of dirt and rubble pinned Marleen to the floor. She was soon covered.

Thunder rumbled above him. He raised his hands. Lightening fell from the sky. It rained down on the army until every single monster was dead.

Mike realized he was floating, glimpsed himself on a shield. He was suspended ten feet in the air, his arms raised crackling with electricity and his eyes were glowing.

The platform was almost ruined and the bodies of dead monsters were everywhere.

Suddenly a growling voice filled the air: "Hail all, Mike, heir to the throne of the Outskirts and son of earth and sky," rumbled Queen Arenes.

Chapter Twenty-Three
A Battle Won

Mike watched in bewilderment as all the storm thons began bowing; he looked at the still struggling form of Marleen.

"Please give up," he pleaded desperately.

"NEVER!" she spat fiercely.

With tears streaming down his face, he raised both hands and brought them down in one fluid motion. Marleen went limp, her eyes rolled back and she didn't move.

Mike landed on the ground and was immediately tackled by Liva. "WE DID IT!" she cried happily.

Mike searched the crowd of storm thons for one person or sorcerer. Hamlin stood out, her hair blowing. Mike ran to her and embraced her fiercely.

"Teach me how to do that," Hamlin murmured in his ear.

Thoran approached him. "Well, you didn't die--that's something," she reprimanded. "Hey, where's Thrisa?" she asked, looking around as if expecting the cheerful little gorglian to pop up any second.

"Um, we lost her," the grief for the little gorglian crashed down on Mike again just as hard.

"WHAT!" exploded Thoran.

Tothan placed a comforting hand on his sister's shoulder.

"Look, Mike. This isn't just about me. Thrisa was the last of her species. The last gorgelina," snapped Thoran. "With her gone, the species is gone," Hamlin cleared her throat but said nothing.

Zareen stepped forward. Blood was trickling from a gash in his cheek but he looked okay. "Mike, tho still not know why thee speak elvish," Zareen growled.

"He has to be an elf," decided Tothan.

"Yes, there is no other possibility," agreed Thoran.

"But Mike cannot be an elf," put in Hamlin. "He is related to Lord Devil, that is his only tie to this world."

The language problem seemed to be the least of his worries. "Worry about that later," Mike called.

"Hey, Mike, can we go home now?" Cand asked. He was up and as lively as usual. Whatever spell Liva used to heal him had worked.

"One sec," Mike muttered. "Hown, how are you in this world?" asked Mike.

Hown shrugged. "Portal," he muttered.

"Speaking of portals, you have to go NOW!" snapped Thoran.

"One more thing, what are you talking about? Ya now heir of Devil?" asked Mike.

"You see, you and Hamlin are the last living heirs to the Outskirts. All the power in Lord Devil is in you. Now that's what we mean by you have reached your prime," explained Thoran.

Mike exchanged a look with Hamlin. "I will be fine," she promised.

Queen Arnes approached him. "Storm thons….. Swore to protect…. Heir of Devil….

That why you no harm by us," the Queen growled as she dipped her head to him and backed away.

Mike looked around at his surroundings and his friends. He embraced everyone.

"Will I ever see you again?" asked Mike.

Hamlin embraced him fiercely. "Count on it," she murmured in his ear.

Mike released Hamlin's arm and he pulled away with Liva at his arm. He turned towards the portal.

"Hown, you coming?" he called, but Hown just shook his head.

"Maybe someday," he called. Mike didn't question it.

"We will see you again," promised Liva.

And they stepped into the portal. All Mike could see were swirls of blue flashing past his eyes. Liva was nowhere to be seen. He let himself have a breath of relief: he was heading back. With a small thrill, he realized that he would see his parents again.

Something jerked him out of his happy thoughts, something horrible.

Without warning, Mike felt a sharp tug on his foot. He didn't know how, but Marleen had grabbed his foot and was dragging him back into the Stanchess.

Epilogue

The night was clear and beautiful with all the stars in view, but it didn't fool the young gorgelina. She knew how dark the world could be.

Jalanas was a young gorgelina on the run. She heard the thud of countless boots. Spreading her small amber wings, she floated into the night. Her fur was coated with mud and her small wings were weary from traveling.

She didn't know what was happening; she just wanted her mother, Thrisa. The little gorgelina was starving and didn't know how to fend for herself, but she knew one thing: things were hunting her.

Jalanas landed on the sodden ground. She shivered as she felt the mud squelch between her talons. She heard the shout of someone coming closer and closer. She huddled together in the wet undergrowth. The shouts were closer than before.

Nearly twenty creatures burst from the bushes surrounding Jalanas. The things wore bright red clothes that covered their entire bodies. They held whips at the ready and one was dragging a large cage. Most of them held torches.

Knowing about species had never really been Janalas strong suit, but she recognized the things right away. They were orpalns, a fearsome species that hunted, captured and then sold unique species, and she was their next target. The orpalns approached her hungrily and Jalanas curled away frightened, but it was too late--they were closing in. Suddenly, out of the corner of her eye, Jalanas saw a bright flash of red.

A young woman appeared. She had long auburn hair and her eyes flashed red. She raised her hands as her eyes shone brighter. Flames blew out of them and turned the orpalns to dust.

Janalas approached cautiously. The woman's eyes stopped glowing and she reached out a hand. Janalas carefully placed her little talon in the woman's hand.

"Hello, little gorgelina, my name is Hamlin. Come, you will be safe with me."

About the Author

E.M Leiva lives in Natick, Massachusetts with her sister and parents. She is currently 10 years old and started her first novel, *The Stanchess*, while she was in lock down and school was virtual in third grade. She loves to explore the deepest depths of fantasy and has been writing since she was very young. She also loves to read as much as she loves to write. She hopes to continue her passion for writing as long as she can.

Synopsis

~When the Devil has brought fire and pain to
the land
Find the girl of the souls with the fire deep
inside her~

When 13 year old Mike Lukowski's
brother is kidnapped by a mysterious
man who appeared out of thin air, he is
plunged into a twist of events that lead
him to another world. Mike struggles to
find his brother before it is too late, but
when an unexpected twist is revealed, he
is forced to make a choice. The choice
will affect the entire world--for good
and for bad. He must decide between
love and family. As the darkest and
deepest secrets are revealed, he is faced
with life and death.

"*The Stanchess* is a refreshing, page-turning debut novel, revealing how young minds are perfectly suited to writing the genre of fantasy." -- High School English Teacher

"E.M. Leiva uncovers her imagination with her characters' entertaining, witty dialogue embedded within an action-packed plot full of suspense and surprises." -- College English Major

"*The Stanchess* is a fun retreat into a new world full of different species and where nothing seems impossible. Bring on *The Stanchess 2*!!!" -- Literature Fan & Avid Book Club Member